DEMONIC, DANGEROUS & DEADLY

DEMONIC, DANGEROUS & DEADLY

AN ANTHOLOGY BY

HELEN HOKE

LODESTAR BOOKS
E. P. DUTTON   NEW YORK

Copyright © 1983 by Helen Hoke

LIBRARY OF CONGRESS CATALOGING IN PUBLICATION DATA

Demonic, dangerous & deadly.
"Lodestar books."
Contents: Lamb to the slaughter / Roald Dahl—A resumed identity / Ambrose Bierce—Waxworks / Robert Bloch—[etc.]
1. Horror tales, American.   2. Horror tales, English.
3. Children's stories, American.   4. Children's stories, English.   [1. Horror—Fiction.   2. Short stories]   I. Hoke, Helen, date.   II. Title: Demonic, dangerous, and deadly.
PZ5.D4   1983   [Fic]   82-17697
ISBN 0-525-67141-2

Published in the United States by E. P. Dutton, Inc., 2 Park Avenue, New York, N.Y. 10016
Published simultaneously in Canada by Clarke, Irwin & Company Limited, Toronto and Vancouver
Editor: Virginia Buckley   Designer: Trish Parcell
Printed in the U.S.A.   First Edition
10 9 8 7 6 5 4 3 2 1

ACKNOWLEDGMENTS

The selections in this book are used by permission of and special arrangements with the proprietors of their respective copyrights, who are listed below. The editor's and publisher's thanks go to all who have made this collection possible.

The editor and publisher have made every effort to trace ownership of all material contained herein. It is their belief that the necessary permissions from the publishers, authors, and authorized agents have been obtained in all cases. In the event of any questions arising as to the use of any material, the editor and publisher express regret for any error unconsciously made and will be pleased to make the necessary corrections in future editions of the book.

"Green Thoughts" by John Collier. Copyright © 1931, 1958 by Harper's Magazine Co. Reprinted by permission of the Harold Matson Company, Inc., New York, and A. D. Peters & Co., Ltd., London.

"Lamb to the Slaughter" by Roald Dahl. Copyright © 1953 by Roald Dahl. Reprinted from *Someone Like You* by Roald Dahl, by permission of Alfred A. Knopf, Inc., and A. Watkins, Inc.

"Man Overboard!" by Winston Churchill. Reprinted by permission of Curtis Brown, Ltd., London and New York.

"The Mistake" by G. Fielden Hughes, from *The First Pan Book of Horror Stories* selected by Herbert van Thal, published by Pan Books Ltd., London.

"Murder and Lonely Hearts" by Helen Nielsen. Reprinted by permission of the author and her agents, the Scott Meredith Literary Agency Inc., 845 Third Avenue, New York, NY 10022, U.S.A.

"So You Won't Talk" by Manuel Komroff, from *The 8th Fontana Book of Great Horror Stories*. Reprinted by permission of Odette Komroff.

"The Tsantsa" by Maurice Sandoz, from *The Eighth Pan Book of Horror Stories* selected by Herbert van Thal, published by Pan Books Ltd., London.

"Waxworks" by Robert Bloch. Reprinted by permission of the author and his agents, the Scott Meredith Literary Agency Inc., 845 Third Avenue, New York, NY 10022, U.S.A.

To Edith Heal Berrien, with love

CONTENTS

ABOUT THIS BOOK

As ALWAYS in my anthologies of horror and the supernatural, a meticulous search was made for the enthralling tales offered in *Demonic, Dangerous and Deadly.*

The superlative roster of writers presented here, and whose toil I trust may draw out some of your own sweat, includes a unique author—Winston Churchill—universally regarded as one of the greatest statesmen of our century. Though he is much admired as a memorable and powerful writer of factual history, the fact that Churchill also wrote fiction remains little known. It is therefore with particular pleasure that a tale by him, first published in 1898, is included herein.

In this anthology, inexplicable and dangerous forces will manifest themselves in all sorts of mind-boggling situations in wildly disparate places. Here you will observe how a person's world may suddenly be turned topsy-turvy, or how fervent expectations may be placed in jeopardy or even be cold-bloodedly thwarted. This is a collection in which life's dark potential lurks on every page.

As an example of what is in store, let us take " 'Man Overboard!' " by Winston Churchill. The protagonist of this impressive little drama is about to experience the shock of terror as he is caught, so to speak, between the devil and the deep blue sea.

In "A Resumed Identity," the disquieting tale by Ambrose Bierce, a wanderer returns to familiar surroundings, and discovers in the process the haunting truth of his exact place in them.

A memorable story is told by Fielden Hughes in "The Mistake." Here, a vicar proceeds to uncover his demon. The shuddering discovery he makes is to haunt him for the rest of his days . . . days that are never to meet the night.

Maurice Sandoz' hair-raising narrative, "The Tsantsa," belies the popular belief that diamonds are a girl's best friend. In this classic tale, *only* a most unusual gift can persuade a capricious girl to continue granting her favors to the man captivated by her charms.

In Roald Dahl's imaginative creation, "Lamb to the Slaughter," nothing could be further from the calmly contented Mrs. Maloney's mind than the unexpected blow that shatters her familial bliss to pieces. What eventually does happen will deal a shock, but not without eliciting a few irrepressible chuckles from the reader.

The fantastic verisimilitude that wax figures bear to living beings in Robert Bloch's enthralling tale, "The Waxworks," may convince that not only a da Vinci can depict faces with smiles so real, so intriguing as to make them unforgettable. Strangely, it is the deadly climax reached during a visit to this museum that lingers in memory.

Sooner or later, most criminals develop the need to confess all. But Handsome Dan, a dangerous convict in Manuel Komroff's blood-freezing tale, "So You Won't Talk," is adamant about keeping his mouth shut forever . . . and almost succeeds.

In Helen Nielsen's grim, yet ingeniously funny tale, "Murder and Lonely Hearts," a married couple, out of mutual disaffection, indulge in harmless pen-pal correspondence . . . to *start* with, that is.

John Collier's gripping tale, "Green Thoughts," takes the reader to a greenhouse whose owner, an amateur orchid grower, unwittingly invites demonic powers to stalk him and members of his household. Can they escape?

I trust the urge has already overcome you to turn to the tales themselves. And if they cause some terror to creep under your skin, indeed, this will be a fine tribute to the masterful writers who created them. In this genre of writing, *to terrify* and *to delight* are, of course, synonymous.

Helen Hoke

DEMONIC, DANGEROUS & DEADLY

LAMB TO THE SLAUGHTER

ROALD DAHL

THE ROOM WAS WARM and clean, the curtains drawn, the two table lamps alight—hers and the one by the empty chair opposite. On the sideboard behind her, two tall glasses, soda water, whiskey. Fresh ice cubes in the Thermos bucket.

Mary Maloney was waiting for her husband to come home from work.

Now and again she would glance up at the clock, but without anxiety, merely to please herself with the thought that each minute gone by made it nearer the time when he would come. There was a slow smiling air about her, and about everything she did. The drop of the head as she bent over her sewing was curiously tranquil. Her skin—for this was her sixth month with child—had acquired a wonderful translucent quality, the mouth was soft, and the eyes, with their new placid look, seemed larger, darker than before.

When the clock said ten minutes to five, she began to listen, and a few moments later, punctually as always, she heard the tires on the gravel outside, and the car door slamming, the footsteps passing the window, the key turning in the lock. She laid aside her sewing, stood up, and went forward to kiss him as he came in.

"Hullo darling," she said.

"Hullo," he answered.

She took his coat and hung it in the closet. Then she walked over and made the drinks, a strongish one for him, a weak one for herself; and soon she was back again in her chair with the sewing, and he in the other, opposite, holding the tall glass with both his hands, rocking it so the ice cubes tinkled against the side.

For her, this was always a blissful time of day. She knew he didn't want to speak much until the first drink was finished, and she, on her side, was content to sit quietly, enjoying his company after the long hours alone in the house. She loved to luxuriate in the presence of this man, and to feel—almost as a sunbather feels the sun—that warm male glow that came out of him to her when they were alone together. She loved him for the way he sat loosely in a chair, for the way he came in a door, or moved slowly across the room with long strides. She loved the intent, far look in his eyes when they rested on her, the funny shape of the mouth, and especially the way he remained silent about his tiredness, sitting still with himself until the whiskey had taken some of it away.

"Tired, darling?"

"Yes," he said. "I'm tired." And as he spoke, he did an unusual thing. He lifted his glass and drained it in one swallow although there was still half of it, at least half of it left. She wasn't really watching him, but she knew what he had done because she heard the ice cubes falling back against the bottom of the empty glass when he lowered his arm. He paused a moment, leaning forward in the chair, then he got up and went slowly over to fetch himself another.

"I'll get it!" she cried, jumping up.

"Sit down," he said.

When he came back, she noticed that the new drink was dark amber with the quantity of whiskey in it.

"Darling, shall I get your slippers?"

"No."

She watched him as he began to sip the dark yellow drink, and she could see little oily swirls in the liquid because it was so strong.

"I think it's a shame," she said, "that when a policeman gets to be as senior as you, they keep him walking about on his feet all day long."

He didn't answer, so she bent her head again and went on with her sewing; but each time he lifted the drink to his lips, she heard the ice cubes clinking against the side of the glass.

"Darling," she said. "Would you like me to get you some cheese? I haven't made any supper because it's Thursday."

"No," he said.

"If you're too tired to eat out," she went on, "it's still not too late. There's plenty of meat and stuff in the freezer, and you can have it right here and not even move out of the chair."

Her eyes waited on him for an answer, a smile, a little nod, but he made no sign.

"Anyway," she went on, "I'll get you some cheese and crackers first."

"I don't want it," he said.

She moved uneasily in her chair, the large eyes still watching his face. "But you *must* have supper. I can easily do it here. I'd like to do it. We can have lamb chops. Or pork. Anything you want. Everything's in the freezer."

"Forget it," he said.

"But darling, you *must* eat! I'll fix it anyway, and then you can have it or not, as you like."

She stood up and placed her sewing on the table by the lamp.

"Sit down," he said. "Just for a minute, sit down."

It wasn't till then that she began to get frightened.

"Go on," he said. "Sit down."

She lowered herself back slowly into the chair, watching him all the time with those large, bewildered eyes. He had finished the second drink and was staring down into the glass, frowning.

"Listen," he said. "I've got something to tell you."

"What is it, darling? What's the matter?"

He had now become absolutely motionless, and he kept his head down so that the light from the lamp beside him fell across the upper part of his face, leaving the chin and mouth in shadow. She noticed there was a little muscle moving near the corner of his left eye.

"This is going to be a bit of a shock to you, I'm afraid," he said. "But I've thought about it a good deal and I've decided the only thing to do is tell you right away. I hope you won't blame me too much."

And he told her. It didn't take long, four or five minutes at most, and she sat very still through it all, watching him with a kind of dazed horror as he went further and further away from her with each word.

"So there it is," he added. "And I know it's kind of a bad time to be telling you, but there simply wasn't any other way. Of course I'll give you money and see you're looked after. But there needn't really be any fuss. I hope not anyway. It wouldn't be very good for my job."

Her first instinct was not to believe any of it, to reject it all. It occurred to her that perhaps he hadn't even spoken, that she herself had imagined the whole thing. Maybe, if she went about her business and acted as though she hadn't been listening, then later, when she sort of woke up again, she might find none of it had ever happened.

"I'll get the supper," she managed to whisper, and this time he didn't stop her.

When she walked across the room, she couldn't feel her feet touching the floor. She couldn't feel anything at all—except a slight nausea and a desire to vomit. Everything was automatic now—down the steps to the cellar, the light switch, the deep freeze, the hand inside the cabinet taking hold of the first object it met. She lifted it out and looked at it. It was wrapped in paper, so she took off the paper and looked at it again.

A leg of lamb.

All right then, they would have lamb for supper. She carried it upstairs, holding the thin bone-end of it with both her hands, and as she went through the living room, she saw him standing over by the window with his back to her, and she stopped.

"For God's sake," he said, hearing her, but not turning around. "Don't make supper for me. I'm going out."

At that point, Mary Maloney simply walked up behind him and without any pause she swung the big frozen leg of lamb high in the air and brought it down as hard as she could on the back of his head.

She might just as well have hit him with a steel club.

She stepped back a pace, waiting, and the funny thing was that he remained standing there for at least four or five seconds, gently swaying. Then he crashed to the carpet.

The violence of the crash, the noise, the small table overturning, helped bring her out of the shock. She came out slowly, feeling cold and surprised, and she stood for a while blinking at the body, still holding the ridiculous piece of meat tight with both hands.

All right, she told herself. So I've killed him.

It was extraordinary, now, how clear her mind became all of a sudden. She began thinking very fast. As the wife of a detective, she knew quite well what the penalty would be. That was fine. It made no difference to her. In fact, it would be a relief. On the other hand, what about the child? What were the laws about murderers with unborn children? Did they kill them both—mother and child? Or did they wait until the tenth month? What did they do?

Mary Maloney didn't know. And she certainly wasn't prepared to take a chance.

She carried the meat into the kitchen, placed it in a pan, turned the oven on high, and shoved it inside. Then she washed her hands and ran upstairs to the bedroom. She sat down before the mirror, tidied her hair, touched up her lips and face. She tried to smile. It came out rather peculiar. She tried again.

"Hullo Sam," she said brightly, aloud.

The voice sounded peculiar too.

"I want some potatoes please, Sam. Yes, and I think a can of peas."

That was better. Both the smile and the voice were coming out better now. She rehearsed it several times more. Then she ran downstairs, took her coat, went out the back door, down the garden, into the street.

It wasn't six o'clock yet and the lights were still on in the grocery shop.

"Hullo Sam," she said brightly, smiling at the man behind the counter.

"Why, good evening, Mrs. Maloney. How're *you?*"

"I want some potatoes please, Sam. Yes, and I think a can of peas."

The man turned and reached up behind him on the shelf for the peas.

"Patrick's decided he's tired and doesn't want to eat out tonight," she told him. "We usually go out Thursdays, you know, and now he's caught me without any vegetables in the house."

"Then how about meat, Mrs. Maloney?"

"No, I've got meat, thanks. I got a nice leg of lamb from the freezer."

"Oh."

"I don't much like cooking it frozen, Sam, but I'm taking a chance on it this time. You think it'll be all right?"

"Personally," the grocer said, "I don't believe it makes any difference. You want these Idaho potatoes?"

"Oh yes, that'll be fine. Two of those."

"Anything else?" The grocer cocked his head on one side, looking at her pleasantly. "How about afterwards? What you going to give him for afterwards?"

"Well—what would you suggest, Sam?"

The man glanced around his shop. "How about a nice big slice of cheesecake? I know he likes that."

"Perfect," she said. "He loves it."

And when it was all wrapped and she had paid, she put on her brightest smile and said, "Thank you, Sam. Good night."

"Good night, Mrs. Maloney. And thank *you*."

And now, she told herself as she hurried back, all she was doing now, she was returning home to her husband and he was waiting for his supper; and she must cook it good, and make it as tasty as possible because the poor man was tired; and if, when she entered the house, she happened to find anything unusual, or tragic, or terrible, then naturally it would be a shock and she'd become frantic with grief and horror. Mind you, she wasn't *expecting* to find anything. She was just going home with the vegetables on Thursday evening to cook supper for her husband.

That's the way, she told herself. Do everything right and natural. Keep things absolutely natural, and there'll be no need for any acting at all.

Therefore, when she entered the kitchen by the back door, she was humming a little tune to herself and smiling.

"Patrick!" she called. "How are you, darling?"

She put the parcel down on the table and went through into the living room; and when she saw him lying there on the floor with his legs doubled up and one arm twisted back underneath his body, it really was rather a shock. All the old love and longing for him welled up inside her, and she ran over to him, knelt down beside him, and began to cry her heart out. It was easy. No acting was necessary.

A few minutes later she got up and went to the phone. She knew the number of the police station, and when the man at the other end answered, she cried to him, "Quick! Come quick! Patrick's dead!"

"Who's speaking?"

"Mrs. Maloney. Mrs. Patrick Maloney."

"You mean Patrick Maloney's dead?"

"I think so," she sobbed. "He's lying on the floor and I think he's dead."

"Be right over," the man said.

The car came very quickly, and when she opened the front door, two policemen walked in. She knew them both—she knew nearly all the men at that precinct—and she fell right into Jack Noonan's arms, weeping hysterically. He put her gently into a chair, then went over to join the other one, who was called O'Malley, kneeling by the body.

"Is he dead?" she cried.

"I'm afraid he is. What happened?"

Briefly, she told her story about going out to the grocer and coming back to find him on the floor. While she was talking, crying and talking, Noonan discovered a small patch of congealed blood on the dead man's head. He showed it to O'Malley, who got up at once and hurried to the phone.

Soon, other men began to come into the house. First a doctor, then two detectives, one of whom she knew by name. Later, a police photographer arrived and took pictures, and a man who knew about fingerprints. There was a great deal of whispering and muttering beside the corpse, and the detectives kept asking her a lot of questions. But they always treated her kindly. She told her story again, this time right from the beginning, when Patrick had come in, and she was sewing, and he was tired, so tired he hadn't wanted to go out for supper. She told how she'd put the meat in the oven—"It's there now, cooking"—and how she'd slipped out to the grocer for vegetables, and come back to find him lying on the floor.

"Which grocer?" one of the detectives asked.

She told him, and he turned and whispered something to the other detective, who immediately went outside into the street.

In fifteen minutes he was back with a page of notes, and there was more whispering, and through her sobbing she heard a few of the whispered phrases—". . . acted quite normal . . . very cheerful . . . wanted to give him a good supper . . . peas . . . cheesecake . . . impossible that she . . ."

After a while, the photographer and the doctor departed, and two other men came in and took the corpse away on a stretcher.

Then the fingerprint man went away. The two detectives remained, and so did the two policemen. They were exceptionally nice to her, and Jack Noonan asked if she wouldn't rather go somewhere else, to her sister's house perhaps, or to his own wife, who would take care of her and put her up for the night.

No, she said. She didn't feel she could move even a yard at the moment. Would they mind awfully if she stayed just where she was until she felt better? She didn't feel too good at the moment, she really didn't.

Then hadn't she better lie down on the bed? Jack Noonan asked.

No, she said. She'd like to stay right where she was, in this chair. A little later perhaps, when she felt better, she would move.

So they left her there while they went about their business, searching the house. Occasionally one of the detectives asked her another question. Sometimes Jack Noonan spoke to her gently as he passed by. Her husband, he told her, had been killed by a blow on the back of the head administered with a heavy blunt instrument, almost certainly a large piece of metal. They were looking for the weapon. The murderer may have taken it with him, but on the other hand he may've thrown it away or hidden it somewhere on the premises.

"It's the old story," he said. "Get the weapon, and you've got the man."

Later, one of the detectives came up and sat beside her. Did she know, he asked, of anything in the house that could've been used as the weapon? Would she mind having a look around to see if anything was missing—a very big wrench, for example, or a heavy metal vase.

They didn't have any heavy metal vases, she said.

"Or a big wrench?"

She didn't think they had a big wrench. But there might be some things like that in the garage.

The search went on. She knew that there were other policemen in the garden all around the house. She could hear their footsteps on the gravel outside, and sometimes she saw the flash of a torchlight through a chink in the curtains. It began to get late, nearly nine she noticed by the clock on the mantle. The four men searching the rooms seemed to be growing weary, a trifle exasperated.

"Jack," she said, the next time Sergeant Noonan went by. "Would you mind giving me a drink?"

"Sure I'll give you a drink. You mean this whiskey?"

"Yes please. But just a small one. It might make me feel better."

He handed her the glass.

"Why don't you have one yourself?" she said. "You must be awfully tired. Please do. You've been very good to me."

"Well," he answered. "It's not strictly allowed, but I might take just a drop to keep me going."

One by one, the others came in and were persuaded to take a little nip of whiskey. They stood around rather awkwardly with the drinks in their hands, uncomfortable in her presence, trying to say consoling things to her. Sergeant Noonan wandered into the kitchen, came out quickly and said, "Look, Mrs. Maloney. You know that oven of yours is still on, and the meat still inside."

"Oh *dear* me!" she cried. "So it is!"

"I'd better turn it off for you, hadn't I?"

"Will you do that, Jack? Thank you so much."

When the sergeant returned the second time, she looked at him with her large, dark, tearful eyes. "Jack Noonan," she said.

"Yes?"

"Would you do me a small favor—you and these others?"

"We can try, Mrs. Maloney."

"Well," she said. "Here you all are, and good friends of dear Patrick's too, and helping to catch the man who killed him. You must be terribly hungry by now because it's long past your suppertime, and I know Patrick would never forgive me, God bless his soul, if I allowed you to remain in his house without offering you decent hospitality. Why don't you eat up the lamb that's in the oven? It'll be cooked just right by now."

"Wouldn't dream of it," Sergeant Noonan said.

"Please," she begged. "Please eat it. Personally, I couldn't touch a thing, certainly not what's been in the house when he was here. But it's all right for you. It'd be a favor to me if you'd eat it up. Then you can go on with your work again afterwards."

There was a good deal of hesitating among the four policemen, but they were clearly hungry, and in the end they were persuaded to go into the kitchen and help themselves. The woman stayed where she was, listening to them through the open door, and she could hear them speaking among themselves, their voices thick and sloppy because their mouths were full of meat.

"Have some more, Charlie?"

"No. Better not finish it."

"She *wants* us to finish it. She said so. Be doing her a favor."

"Okay then. Give me some more."

"That's a hell of a big club the guy must've used to hit poor Patrick," one of them was saying. "The doc says his skull was smashed all to pieces just like from a sledgehammer."

"That's why it ought to be easy to find."

"Exactly what I say."

"Whoever done it, they're not going to be carrying a thing like that around with them longer than they need to."

One of them belched.

"Personally, I think it's right here on the premises."

"Probably right under our very noses. What'd you think, Jack?"

And in the other room, Mary Maloney began to giggle.

A RESUMED IDENTITY

AMBROSE BIERCE

1

ONE SUMMER NIGHT a man stood on a low hill overlooking a wide expanse of forest and field. By the full moon hanging low in the west, he knew what he might not have known otherwise: that it was near the hour of dawn. A light mist lay along the earth, partly veiling the lower features of the landscape, but above it the taller trees showed in well-defined masses against a clear sky. Two or three farmhouses were visible through the haze, but in none of them, naturally, was a light. Nowhere, indeed, was any sign or suggestion of life except the barking of a distant dog, which, repeated with mechanical iteration, served rather to accentuate than dispel the loneliness of the scene.

The man looked curiously about him on all sides, as one who among familiar surroundings is unable to determine his exact place and part in the scheme of things. It is so, perhaps, that we shall act when, risen from the dead, we await the call to judgment.

A hundred yards away was a straight road, showing white in the moonlight. Endeavoring to orient himself, as a surveyor or navigator might say, the man moved his eyes slowly along its visible length, and at a distance of a quarter-mile to the south of his station saw, dim and gray in the haze, a group of horsemen riding to the north. Behind them were men afoot, marching in column, with dimly gleaming rifles aslant above their shoulders. They moved slowly and in silence. Another group of horsemen, another regiment of infantry, another and another—all in unceasing motion toward the man's point of view, past it, and beyond. A battery of artillery followed, the cannoneers riding with folded arms on limber and caisson. And still the interminable procession came out of the obscurity to the south and passed into the obscurity to the north, with never a sound of voice, nor hoof nor wheel.

The man could not rightly understand. He thought himself deaf, said so, and heard his own voice, although it had an unfamiliar quality that almost alarmed him; it disappointed his ear's expectancy in the matter of timbre and resonance. But he was not deaf, and that for the moment sufficed.

Then he remembered that there are natural phenomena to which someone has given the name "acoustic shadows." If you stand in an acoustic shadow, there is one direction from which you will hear nothing. At the battle of Gaines's Mill, one of the fiercest conflicts of the Civil War, with a hundred guns in play, spectators a mile and a half away on the opposite side of the Chickahominy Valley heard nothing of what they clearly saw. The bombardment of Port Royal, heard and felt at St. Augustine, a hundred and fifty miles to the south, was inaudible two miles to the north in a still atmosphere. A few days before the surrender at Appomattox, a thunderous engagement between the commands of Sheridan and Pickett was unknown to the latter commander, a mile in the rear of his own line.

These instances were not known to the man of whom we write, but less striking ones of the same character had not escaped his observation. He was profoundly disquieted, but for another reason than the uncanny silence of that moonlight march.

"Good Lord!" he said to himself—and again it was as if another had spoken his thought—"if those people are what I take them to be we have lost the battle and they are moving on Nashville!"

Then came a thought of self—an apprehension—a strong sense of personal peril, such as in another we call fear. He stepped quickly into the shadow of a tree. And still the silent battalions moved slowly forward in the haze.

The chill of a sudden breeze upon the back of his neck drew his attention to the quarter whence it came, and turning to the east, he saw a faint gray light along the horizon—the first sign of returning day. This increased his apprehension.

"I must get away from here," he thought, "or I shall be discovered and taken."

He moved out of the shadow, walking rapidly toward the graying east. From the safer seclusion of a clump of cedars, he looked back. The entire column had passed out of sight: The straight white road lay bare and desolate in the moonlight!

Puzzled before, he was now inexpressibly astonished. So swift a passing of so slow an army!—he could not comprehend it. Minute after minute passed unnoted; he had lost his sense of time. He sought with a terrible earnestness a solution of the mystery, but sought in vain. When at last he roused himself from his abstraction, the sun's rim was visible above the hills, but in the new conditions he found no other light than that of day; his understanding was involved as darkly in doubt as before.

On every side lay cultivated fields showing no sign of war and war's ravages. From the chimneys of the farmhouses, thin ascensions of blue smoke signalled preparations for a day's peaceful toil. Having stilled its immemorial allocution to the moon, the watchdog was assisting a Negro who, prefixing a team of mules to the plough, was flatting and sharping at his task. The hero of this tale stared stupidly at the pastoral picture as if he had never seen such a thing in all his life; then he put his hand to his head, passed it through his hair and, withdrawing it, attentively considered the palm—a singular thing to do. Apparently reassured by the act, he walked confidently toward the road.

2

Dr. Stilling Malson, of Murfreesboro, having visited a patient six or seven miles away, on the Nashville road, had remained with him all night. At daybreak he set out for home on horseback, as was the custom of doctors of the time and region. He had passed into the neighborhood of Stones River battlefield when a man approached him from the roadside and saluted in the military fashion, with a movement of the right hand to the hat brim. But the hat was not a military hat, the man was not in uniform and had not a martial bearing. The doctor nodded civilly, half thinking that the stranger's uncommon greeting was perhaps in deference to the historic surroundings. As the stranger evidently desired speech with him, he courteously reined in his horse and waited.

"Sir," said the stranger, "although a civilian, you are perhaps an enemy."

"I am a physician," was the non-committal reply.

"Thank you," said the other. "I am a lieutenant of the staff of General Hazen." He paused a moment and looked sharply at the person whom he was addressing, then added, "Of the Federal army."

The physician merely nodded.

"Kindly tell me," continued the other, "what has happened here. Where are the armies? Which has won the battle?"

The physician regarded his questioner curiously with half-shut eyes. After a professional scrutiny, prolonged to the limit of politeness, "Pardon me," he said, "one asking information should be willing to impart it. Are you wounded?" he added, smiling.

"Not seriously—it seems."

The man removed the unmilitary hat, put his hand to his head, passed it through his hair, and, withdrawing it, attentively considered the palm.

"I was struck by a bullet and have been unconscious. It must have been a light, glancing blow: I find no blood and feel no pain. I will not trouble you for treatment, but will you kindly direct me to my command—to any part of the Federal army—if you know?"

Again the doctor did not immediately reply: He was recalling much that is recorded in the books of his profession—something about lost identity and the effect of familiar scenes in restoring it. At length he looked the man in the face, smiled, and said:

"Lieutenant, you are not wearing the uniform of your rank and service."

At this the man glanced down at his civilian attire, lifted his eyes, and said with hesitation:

"That is true. I—I don't quite understand."

Still regarding him sharply but not unsympathetically, the man of science bluntly inquired:

"How old are you?"

"Twenty-three—if that has anything to do with it."

"You don't look it; I should hardly have guessed you to be just that."

The man was growing impatient. "We need not discuss that," he said. "I want to know about the army. Not two hours ago, I saw a column of troops moving northward on this road. You must have met them. Be good enough to tell me the color of their clothing, which I was unable to make out, and I'll trouble you no more."

"You are quite sure that you saw them?"

"Sure? My God, sir, I could have counted them!"

"Why, really," said the physician, with an amusing consciousness of his own resemblance to the loquacious barber of *The Arabian Nights,* "this is very interesting. I met no troops."

The man looked at him coldly, as if he had himself observed the likeness to the barber. "It is plain," he said, "that you do not care to assist me. Sir, you may go to the devil!"

He turned and strode away, very much at random, across the dewy fields, his half-penitent tormentor quietly watching him from his point of vantage in the saddle till he disappeared beyond an array of trees.

3

After leaving the road, the man slackened his pace, and now went forward, rather deviously, with a distinct feeling of fatigue. He could not account for this, though truly the interminable loquacity of that country doctor offered itself in explanation. Seating himself upon a rock, he laid one hand upon his knee, back upward, and casually looked at it. It was lean and withered. He lifted both hands to his face. It was seamed and furrowed; he could trace the lines with the tips of his fingers. How strange!— a mere bullet-stroke and a brief unconsciousness should not make one a physical wreck.

"I must have been a long time in the hospital," he said aloud. "Why, what a fool I am! The battle was in December, and it is now summer." He laughed. "No wonder that fellow thought me an escaped lunatic. He was wrong: I am only an escaped patient."

At a little distance a small plot of ground enclosed by a stone wall caught his attention. With no very definite intent, he rose and went to it. In the center was a square, solid monument of hewn stone. It was brown with age, weather-worn at the angles, spotted with moss and lichen. Between the massive blocks were strips of grass, the leverage of whose roots had pushed them apart. In answer to the challenge of this ambitious structure, Time had laid his destroying hand upon it, and it would soon be "one with Nineveh and Tyre." In an inscription on one side, his eye caught a familiar name. Shaking with excitement, he craned his body across the wall and read:

HAZEN'S BRIGADE
TO
THE MEMORY OF ITS SOLDIERS
WHO FELL AT
STONES RIVER, DEC. 31, 1862

The man fell back from the wall, faint and sick. Almost within an arm's length was a little depression in the earth; it had been filled by a recent rain—a pool of clear water. He crept to it to revive himself, lifted the upper part of his body on his trembling arms, thrust forward his head and saw the reflection of his face, as in a mirror. He uttered a terrible cry. His arms gave way; he fell, face downward, into the pool and yielded up the life that had spanned another life.

WAXWORKS

ROBERT BLOCH

1

IT HAD BEEN A DULL DAY for Bertrand before his discovery of
the waxworks—a dark, foggy day which he had spent in tramping
aimlessly about the dingy streets of the quay district he loved. It
had been a dull day, but none the less it was of a sort that Bertrand's
imaginative nature best loved. He found a morose enjoyment in
the feel of the stinging sleet upon his face, liked, too, the sensation
of semi-blindness induced by the nebulosity of outline conjured
up with the fog. Mist made the dingy buildings and the narrow
streets that threaded crookedly between them seem unreal and
grotesque; the commonplace stone structures squatted in blueness
like vast, inanimate monsters carven from cyclopean stone.

So, at least, thought Bertrand, in his somewhat maudlin fashion.
For Bertrand was a poet—a very bad poet, with the sentimentally
esoteric nature such beings affect. He lived in a garret in the dock
district, ate crusts of bread, and fancied himself very much put

upon by the world. In moments of self-pity, which were frequent, he made certain mental comparisons between his estate and that of the late François Villon. These estimates were none too flattering to the latter gentleman; for after all, Villon had been a pimp and a thief, whereas Bertrand was neither. Bertrand was just a very honorable young man whom people had not yet learned to appreciate, and if he starved now, posterity would spread him a pretty feast. So his thoughts ran a good part of the time, and days of fog like this were ideal for such personal compassions. It was warm enough in Bertrand's garret, and there was food there, for after all, his parents in Marseilles did send him money regularly, under the impression that he was a student at the college. Yes, the garret was a fine refuge on such a dismal afternoon, and Bertrand could have been hard at work on one of those noble sonnets he was always intending to produce. But no, he must wander about in the fog, and think things out for himself. It was so—romantic—he grudgingly conceded, in his mind, for he hated to use "trite" expressions.

This "romantic" phase was beginning to pall on the young man after an hour's walk about the wharves; sleet and drizzling rain had dampened more than his ardor. Then too, he had just discovered in himself a most unpoetic case of the snuffles.

In consequence, he was more than heartened by the sight of the dim lamp that shone through the murk from a dark basement doorway between two houses on this obscure side street. The lantern served to illuminate a sign proclaiming WAXWORKS WITHIN.

Upon reading this legend, Bertrand felt a faint tinge of disappointment. He had hoped that the beacon ornamented the door of a tavern, for our poet was given to the bottle at those odd times when he found himself in funds. None the less, the light was a symbol of warmth and shelter within, and perhaps the waxworks would be interesting.

He went down the steps, opened the dark door, and stepped, shivering slightly at the sudden change, into a warm, dimly lit hallway.

A fat little man in a greasy cap shuffled out from behind a side door and took his three francs with a shrug of surprise, as if wordlessly indicating his amazement at securing a customer at such a time.

Bertrand glanced down the plain hall as he removed his wet jacket. His fastidious nose wrinkled slightly at the musty odor about the place; this, combined with the peculiar acridity common only to discarded wet garments in a warm room, gave the air a genuine "museum smell."

As he walked down the hall to the wide doorway leading into the exhibit, he was conscious of a subtle heightening of his melancholy, which the fog had so visibly augmented. Here in this shabby darkness he felt a profound spiritual depression. Without knowing it, he slipped from self-dramatization into reality. His mind craved morbidity; his thoughts were steeped in umber stillness . . . *steeped in umber stillness* . . . he must remember that, and write it down.

He was, in point of fact, quite properly in the mood for the waxworks exhibit which he now beheld. It was a carnival of the gruesome and the macabre.

Once, in a moment of temporary affluence, Bertrand and a feminine companion had visited the great Madame Tussaud's. His memories of the occasion were vague and dealt more fully with the charms of the young lady than with the rather inanimate attractions of the statuary. But as he recalled it, the wax figures had been those of historically prominent and journalistically notorious personages: representations of generals and statesmen and movie stars. This had been Bertrand's sole experience in viewing such objects, save for the odious Punch and Judy displays in the traveling carnival companies he visited during his far-off childhood. (He was twenty-three.)

A casual glance served to show that these waxworks were of a vastly different nature.

A long vast chamber stretched before him—a surprisingly large chamber for such an obscure enterprise, he thought. It was low-ceilinged, and the fog outside the narrow windows lent an effective dimness to the already poor lighting arrangements, so that the atmosphere was one of profound gloom appropriate to the scene.

An army of still white figures paraded in arrested processional against the dingy walls—an army of stiffly staring corpses—an army of *mummified, embalmed, petrified, ossified* . . . he ran out of descriptive terminology and realized guiltily that his words were pitifully inadequate to describe the impressiveness of these silent wax figures. They held an attitude of arrested motion which in turn captured a peculiar feeling of ominous *waiting*. They seemed to have just died; or rather to have been frozen in some airy, invisible ice that was about to melt and release them once again at any moment.

For they were realistic. And the lighting effects of the room disguised what crudities and blemishes might exist. Bertrand began to walk along the left wall and gazed intently at each figure or group of figures.

The subject-matter of these exhibits was harrowing in the extreme. Crime was the theme—perverse and dreadful crime. The monster Landru crept upon his sleeping wife in the night, and see, the maniac Tolours lurks with bloody knife behind the barrels as his tiny son descends the cellar stairs. Three men sit within an open boat, and one is armless, legless, headless, while the others feast . . . Gilles de Retz stands before the altar, and his beard is dabbled red as he holds his basin high; the sacrifice lies broken at his feet . . . a woman writhes upon the wheel and the sharp-fanged rats race round and round the dungeon floor . . . flayed alive is he that hangs upon the gibbet, and giant Dessalines advances with a leaded whip . . . the murderer Vardac stands accused while from his suitcase trickles a red stain . . . the fat monk Omelée digs within his crypt amidst the barrels of bones. . . . Here sleeping Evil rises from hidden depths in men's souls and slyly grins.

Bertrand saw and shuddered. There was a disturbingly artful verisimilitude in the depiction of these frights which made him ill at ease. They were so cunningly, so artfully conceived! The details of background and setting seemed minutely authentic, and the figures themselves seemed to be the products of a master craftsmanship. Their simulation of life was startling; their molder had instilled genuine action into pose and posture, so that each pictured movement was actually portrayed. And the heads, with the expressions on the faces, were astonishingly real. They glared and twisted with rage, lust, anger; contorted and blenched with fear, shock, agony. The eyes stared with a more than glassy reality, the hair hung naturally from bearded cheeks, lips opened as though warm with breath.

So they stood, the waxworks figures, each living eternally the supreme moment of the horror which justified their existence as images and damned their souls as living men.

Bertrand saw them all. Little signs proclaimed the characters in each pictured melodrama in suitably grandiloquent style, and cards recited bloody histories of famous misdeeds.

Bertrand read them self-consciously. He knew that what he saw was cheapest theatricalism, sensational yellow-journal stuff at its worst; the type of lurid gore-parading in which the moron-mind delights. But he fancied that there was something rather grand about this whole insane array of melodramatics; they seemed to have a certain *intensity* which ordinary life shuns to express in daily actions. He wondered as he stared whether or not this feeling of intensity was one of the attractions for the ordinary foolish sensation-hunters; whether or not they felt it, and were vaguely envious of its contrast to their sedulously eventless lives. And he almost chuckled when he realized that the pictured scenes were real; that their counterparts had actually existed—moreover, were still existing today, in a hundred hidden places. Yes, murderers and rapists and mad fiends crouched unknown even now, waiting to strike. Some of them would be exposed, others die in secrecy inviolate; but their deeds went on—their gory, melodramatic deeds.

The young poet walked on. He was all alone in this room, and the sight of the blue fog-fingers still clawing at the window-panes encouraged him to take his leisure. He spent much time in noting the perfections of the figures. Gradually he approached the right wall of the hall, which seemed to be given over to the bloody scenes of actual recorded history; the burnings, pillagings, tortures and massacres of olden times. Here too he was forced to concede admiration for the designers of the displays; historical costuming was splendid throughout. There must be many details to this wax-work-making business, he thought, as he examined a particularly noteworthy figure of the Emperor Tiberius Caesar at sport in the torture chamber.

Then he saw her. She was standing statue-still, straight and poised and lovely. She was girl, woman, goddess, imperially slender, with the delicious curves of a succubus fashioned in dreams.

Bertrand's poet-eyes deigned to notice actual physical details, though his bemused brain must translate them anew into elaborate imagery. Thus her splendid auburn hair was a crimson cloud, her smiling, finely chiseled face a mask of enchantment, her starry blue eyes twin pools in which a soul must drown. Her parted lips were curved as though in voluptuous delight, and from them her tongue protruded like a little red dagger whose stab was joy. She wore a filmy, bejeweled robe of sorts, which only served to accentuate the white beauty of the body it half revealed beneath.

Actually, she was a very pretty red-headed woman, and she was wax—common, ordinary wax, very much of the sort which had served to fashion the form of Jack the Ripper. Her pose was commonplace, but arresting; she stood tiptoe with outstretched arms that held a silver salver; stood before King Herod on his throne. For she was Salome, wanton of the seven veils, white witch and wooer of all evil.

Bertrand stared into her wicked oval face, the eyes of which seemed to flicker with amusement in returning his gaze. And he thought that she was the most beautiful creature he had ever beheld, and the most dreadful. Her slim hands held a silver platter, and on it rested the severed head . . . the gory, decapitated head of John the Baptist, lying with stony eyes, death-bright in a pool of blood.

Bertrand didn't move. He simply looked at the woman. A queer impulse to address her came over him. She was mocking his goggle-eyed gazings, she thought him rude. Speak, man! He wanted to tell her—that he loved her.

Bertrand realized this with a thrill of pain that was almost horror. He *did* love her, love her wildly beyond all dreams of love. He wanted her—this woman who was only wax. It was torture to look at her, the ache of her beauty was intolerable when he realized that she was unattainable. What irony! To fall in love with a wax-work!—he must be mad.

But how poetic it was, Bertrand pondered. And not so highly original at that.

He'd read of similar cases, seen some claptrap dramatizations of the theme, which was as old as Pygmalion and his statue.

Reason wouldn't help him, he realized with a sort of despair. He loved her beauty and her menace, always would. He was that sort of poet.

It was amazing, finally to glance up and see the sun sullenly shining through the windows from which fog had fled. How long had he been gaping here? Bertrand turned away, after one last soul-wrenching look at the object of his adoration.

"I'll come back," he whispered. Then he blushed guiltily to himself and hurried down the hall to the door.

2

He came back the next day. And the next. He became familiar with the pudgy gray features of the little fat man who seemed to be the sole attendant at the door; grew to know the dusty museum and its contents. He learned that visitors were scarce these days, and discovered late afternoon was the ideal time for his hours of worship.

For worship it was. He would stand silently before the cryptically smiling statue, and stare enraptured into the maddening cruelty of her eyes. Sometimes he would mumble bits of the verse with which he struggled by night; often he would plead mad lover's entreaties meant for waxen ears. But red-haired Salome only stared back at him in return and regarded his ravings with a set and cryptic smile.

It was odd that he never inquired about the statue or any of the others until the day he spoke with the little fat attendant.

The squat, gray-haired man approached him one day at twilight and entered into conversation, thus ending a revery in a manner which greatly annoyed the love-sick Bertrand.

"Pretty, eh?" said the gray-haired man, in the coarse vulgar voice such unfeeling dolts habitually possess. "I modeled her from my wife, y'know."

His *wife. His* wife—this shabby little old fat fool? Bertrand felt that he was really going mad, until the next words of his companion dispelled the notion.

"Years ago, of course."

But she was alive—real—alive! His heart leaped.

"Yes. She's dead a long time now, of course."

Dead! Gone, as far away as ever, only this taunting waxen shell remaining. Bertrand must talk to this little fool, draw him out. There was so much he had to know. But in a moment he found that there was no need to "draw out" his companion; loneliness evidently begot garrulity upon the little man's part. He mumbled on in his gruff, crude fashion.

"Clever work, isn't it?" The gray-haired dolt was surveying the wax figure in a manner which Bertrand found peculiarly repulsive. There was in his eyes no adoration for the being represented; only the unfeeling appraisal of a craftsman commenting on his handiwork. He was admiring the wax, not the woman.

"My best," mused the little man.

And to think that he had once possessed *her*! . . . Bertrand was sickened dreadfully at the fellow's callousness. But the man did not seem to notice. He kept glancing from the statue to Bertrand and back again. Meanwhile keeping up a steady stream of comment and information.

Monsieur must be interested in the museum, eh? He seemed to be a frequent visitor. Good work, wasn't it? He, Pierre Jacquelin, had done it all. Yes, he had learned the waxworks business well in the past eight years. It cost money to hire assistants; so save for occasional group-pieces, Jacquelin had fashioned all the figures himself. People had done him the honor of favorably comparing his work to Tussaud's. No doubt he could get a place on the staff there, but he preferred to run a quiet business of his own. Besides, there was less notoriety. But the figures were good, weren't they? That's where his medical knowledge served him. Yes, it had been Doctor Jacquelin in the old days.

Monsieur admired his wife, didn't he? Well, that was not strange—there had been others. They too came regularly. No—no need to take offense. It would be silly to be jealous of a wax image. But it was peculiar the way men still came, some of them not even knowing about the crime.

The crime?

Something in the little man's gray face as he mentioned it caused Bertrand to perk up his ears, to ask questions. The old fellow showed no hesitation in answering.

"Can it be that you do not know?" he said. "Ah well, time passes and one forgets the newspapers. It was not a pleasant thing—I wanted to be alone then, and the notoriety caused me to abandon practice. That is how I began here: to get away from it all. *She* caused it."

[31]

He pointed at the statue.

"The Jacquelin case, they called it—because of my wife, you know. I knew nothing until the trial. She was young, alone in Paris when I married her. I knew nothing of her past. I had my practice, I was busy, away a great deal of the time. I never suspected. She was pathological, Monsieur. I had suspected certain things from her conduct, but I loved her and never guessed.

"I brought a patient to the house—an old man. He was quite ill, and she nursed him very devotedly. One night I came in quite late and found him dead. She had cut his throat with a surgical knife—I came upon her silently, you understand—and she was attempting to go further.

"The police took her away. At the trial it all came out; about the young fellow at Brest she had done in, and the two husbands she had disposed of at Lyons and Liège. And she confessed to other crimes; five in all. Decapitation.

"Oh, I was broken up over it, I can tell you! That was years ago, and I was younger then. I loved her, and when she admitted that she had planned to finish me off next I felt—well, never mind. She had been a good wife, you see, quiet and gentle and loving. You can see for yourself how beautiful she was. And to discover that she was mad! A murderess like that . . . it was terrible.

"I did my best. I still wanted her, after all that. It is hard to explain. We tried to plead insanity. But she was convicted, and they sent her to the guillotine."

How badly he tells the story! thought Bertrand. Material for tragedy here, and he bungles it into a farce! When will Life live up to Art?

"My medical practice was ruined, of course. The papers, the publicity, that was fatal. I had lost everything. Then I began this. I'd made plaster busts, medical figures, to earn a little extra through the years. So I took my savings and began the museum.

All these misfortunes had upset me, I can tell you, and I was in a bad way when I started. I had become interested in crime, for obvious reasons. That is why I specialized in this sort of thing."

The little man smiled a bit tolerantly, as though in memory of things long dead and forgotten—emotions. He tapped Bertrand on the chest with a jollity which the latter found hideous.

"What I did was a capital joke, eh? I got permission from the authorities to go down to the morgue. The execution had been delayed and my business here was well started; I had learned my technique. So I went down to the morgue after the guillotining, understand, and made a model of my wife. From life—or death, rather. Yes, I made the model, and it's a grand joke. She had beheaded, and now *she* was beheaded. So why not make her Salome? John the Baptist was beheaded, too, wasn't he? Quite a jest!"

The little man's face fell a bit, and his pale gray eyes grew bright.

"Perhaps it wasn't such a joke, Monsieur. To tell the truth, at the time I did it for revenge. I hated her for the way she had broken my life, hated her because I still loved her in spite of what she had done. And there was more irony than humor in my doings. I wanted her in wax, to stand here and remind me of my life: my love and her crime.

"But that was years ago. The world has forgotten, and I have too. Now she is just a beautiful figure—my best figure.

"Somehow I have never again approached the art, and I think you will agree with me that it is art. I have never achieved such perfection, though I've learned more mastery with the years. Men come in and stare at her, you know, the way you do. I don't believe many of them know the story, but if they did, they would still come. You will come again, won't you—even though you know?"

Bertrand nodded bruskly as he turned and hurried away. He

was playing the fool, rushing out like a child. This he knew, and he cursed himself under his breath even as he ran from the museum and the hateful little old man.

He was a fool. His head throbbed. Why did he hate the man— her husband? Why did he hate her because she had once lived, and killed? If the story were true—and it was. He remembered something of the Jacquelin case, vague headlines dimmed by the passage of years. He'd probably shuddered over the penny-dreadful newspaper versions as a boy. Why did he feel as though he were in torment? A wax statue of a dead murderess, made by her stupid, insensate brute of a husband. Other men came and stared—he hated them, too.

He was losing his mind. This was worse than silly, it was insane. He must never go back there, must forget all about the dead, and the lost that could never be his. Her husband had forgotten, the world had not remembered. Yes. He had made his decision. Never again. . . .

He was very glad that the place was deserted the next day as he prayed before the silent, red-haired beauty of Salome.

3

A few days later, Colonel Bertroux came to his lodging. An insufferable boor, the colonel, a close friend of his family—a retired officer and a born meddler. It did not take Bertrand long to discover that his worried parents had sent the colonel down to "reason" with him.

It was the sort of thing they would do, and the sort of thing a pompous ass like the old colonel would enjoy doing. He was brusk, dignified, pedantic. He called Bertrand "my dear boy" and wasted no time in coming to the point. He wanted Bertrand to give up his "foolishness" and return home to settle down.

The family butcher shop—he belonged there, not in a Paris attic. No, the colonel was not interested in his "poetry scribbling." He came to "reason" with Bertrand.

And more of the same thing, until Bertrand was half frantic with exasperation. He could not insult the old dodderer, try as he may. The man was too stupid to understand his satirical deprecations. He followed Bertrand about the streets when he ate, and took it for granted that he was invited. He "put up" at a nearby hostelry and spent his first night in conversation. He was absurdly confident that "the dear boy" would heed his wisdom.

Bertrand gave up after that evening. The colonel put in his appearance again at noon, just as Bertrand was about to leave for the museum. Despite pointed hints, Colonel Bertroux would be only too glad to accompany him to the waxworks. He did.

Once inside the place, Bertrand sank into the strange mood of mysterious excitement he had now learned to expect—no, to hunger for. The colonel's asinine commentaries on the criminal displays he was able to ignore. His reveries drowned out the conversational background.

They approached *her.* Bertrand said nothing—stood silent on the spot, though his eyes cried out. He gazed, devoured. She mocked. Silently they duelled, as minutes fled down the path of eternity.

Abruptly, Bertrand jerked back to consciousness, blinking like a sleeper just awakened from an enthralling and ecstatic dream. Then he stared.

The colonel was still beside him, and he was gaping at the statue of Salome with utter bemusement. On his face was a look of wonder so alien and somehow youthful that Bertrand was amazed. The man was fascinated—as fascinated as he was!

The colonel? It was impossible! He couldn't have—not he. But he had. He was. He felt it, loved her too!

Bertrand wanted to laugh, at first. But as he looked into that

[35]

utterly absorbed old face once again he felt that tears might be more appropriate. He understood. There was something about this woman that called forth the dreams buried in the soul of every man, old or young. She was so gorgeously aloof, so wickedly wanton.

Bertrand glanced again at her evil tenderness, noted the shapely grace with which she stood holding that horrid head.

That horrid head—it was different, today. Not the black-haired, blue-eyed, glassy-staring head he had seen on previous visits. What was wrong?

A touch on his shoulder. The little gray-haired owner of the waxworks, horribly solicitous.

"Noticed it, eh?" he mumbled. "Deplorable accident; the old head was accidentally broken. One of her—her gentlemen friends tried to poke it with an umbrella, and it fell. I substituted this while repairing the original. But it does detract."

Colonel Bertroux had glanced up from his shattered reveries. The little gray-haired man fawned on him.

"Pretty, eh?" he began. "I modeled her from my wife, y'know."

And he proceeded to tell the whole grim story, just as Bertrand had it from him a week before. He told it just as badly, and in practically the same words.

Bertrand watched the sick-hurt look on the colonel's face, and wondered with a start if he had not appeared much the same way when he listened for the first time.

In curious parallel to his own behavior, it was the colonel who turned on his heel and walked away at the conclusion of the narrative. Bertrand followed, feeling the eyes of the little gray man appraising their departing backs in a quizzical fashion.

They reached the street and walked in silence. The colonel's face still wore t' at dazed expression. At the door of his lodging, the colonel turned to him. His voice was curiously hushed.

"I—I think I'm beginning to understand, my boy. I'll not trouble you again. I'm going back."

He marched up the street, shoulders strangely erect, leaving Bertrand to ponder.

Not a word about the waxworks incident. Nothing! But he loved her too. Strange—the whole affair was strange. Was the colonel going away or *fleeing*?

The little man had retold his story with such curious readiness. It was almost as though he had rehearsed it. Could it be that the entire business was a hoax of some sort? Perhaps it was all a fabrication, a clever ruse on the part of the museum keeper.

Yes, that must be the explanation. Some artist had sold him the wax figure; he noted that its realistic beauty attracted lonely men, and concocted the story of a notorious murderess to fit the statue's history. The case might be real enough, but the little man did not look as though he had ever been the husband of a murderess. Not *her* husband. The story was just bait, a lure to keep the men coming, keep their money rolling in. With a start, Bertrand computed the amount in francs he had spent visiting the museum these past weeks. It was considerable. Clever schemer!

Still, the real attraction lay in the statue itself. The figure was so beautiful, so *alive* in its loveliness, through which there breathed a sort of alluring wickedness. Salome was a red witch, and there was a mystery in her which Bertrand felt he was soon to penetrate. He had to understand that smile and its spell over him. . . .

So thinking, he retired. And the next few days he wrote. He started an epic poem of surprising promise, and labored without pause. He was thankful the colonel had left; grateful to *her* for helping. Perhaps she did understand; perhaps she was real; mayhap she heard his wild mutterings in the night, his lonely entreaties cast up to the stars. Perchance in some far-off poet's Avalon she waited, or in some flaming poet's Hell. He would find her. . . .

He told her that the next day when he thanked her for removing Colonel Bertroux. He was going to recite to her a stanza of his sonnet when he became aware that the eyes of the museum keeper rested on him from a distance down the hall.

He ceased his mutterings, crimson with shame. Spying on him? How often had he gloated over the anguish of the poor wretches enmeshed in her beauty? Withered little beast!

Bertrand tried to look away. He stared at the new head of John the Baptist. Substitute, eh? He wondered under what circumstances the original had been cracked. Some fool with an umbrella, the little man had said. Trying to touch her—as though such a desire were granted a mere mortal! This substitute head was fine, though, as realistic as the first. The closed eyes of the blond young man lent a rather morbid note lacking in the pallid stare of the other. Still, it was not exactly John the Baptist. Hmmm.

The little man was still staring. Bertrand cursed under his breath and turned away. No more peace today. He hurried down the hall, trying to appear oblivious. As he neared the door, he bent his head and sought to avoid the stare of the keeper. In doing so he almost ran into the oncoming figure of a visitor. He muttered a hasty "Your pardon, please" and left. Turning back he gazed with a shock at the retreating back of the man he had jostled.

Was he mad, or did he perceive the shoulders of Colonel Bertroux?

But Bertroux had left—or had he? Was he lured back to worship in privacy, as Bertrand worshiped, as others did? Would the little old man stare at him? Had Salome ensnared another?

Bertrand wondered. The next few days he came at odd hours, hoping to encounter the colonel. He was interested. He wanted to question the older man, seek to learn if he too were affected by this puzzling infatuation for a waxen image.

Bertrand could have questioned the little gray museum keeper concerning his friend, but he felt a vague dislike for the fellow which restrained him. If the keeper's story were a hoax, he hated the imposture; if true, he could not forgive him for having known, for having embraced a beauty Bertrand would have given his life to possess.

The poet left the museum in a state of mental anguish. He hated the place, hated its keeper, hated *her* because his love chained him. Must he come to this dark old dungeon forever, mutely suffering away his life for a glimpse of beauty forever denied him? Must he walk past mocking murderers in gloom to gaze into the eyes of his waxen tormentress? How long? The mystery was unseating his reason. How long?

Wearily he climbed the steps to his room. His key turned in the lock, his door opened on lighted brilliance, and he stepped forward in surprise to confront—Colonel Bertroux.

The old man was seated in the easy-chair, his elbows resting on the table as he faced the poet.

"Pardon this intrusion, boy," said the colonel. "I used a skeleton key to enter. I could have waited outside for you, but I prefer remaining someplace where I am locked in."

His voice was so grave and his face so serious as he spoke these last words that Bertrand accepted their import without questioning.

He framed a reply; he wanted to inquire why Bertroux had not left town, if it had indeed been he whom the poet had seen leaving the museum a few hours previous. But the older man lifted a hand in a tired gesture and motioned Bertrand to a seat on the couch. His dim blue eyes stared out from a face lined with exhaustion.

"Let me explain this visit," he began. "But first, a few questions. I beg of you to answer these truthfully, my boy. Much depends on your veracity, as you shall learn."

Bertrand nodded, impressed by the utter gravity of his visitor.

"First," said the colonel, "I want to know just how long you have been visiting that wax museum."

"About a month. In fact, a month ago tomorrow I made my initial visit."

"And just how did you come to go there, of all places?"

Bertrand explained the circumstances of the fog, the chance glimpse of the sign with its hint of shelter. The colonel listened intently.

"Did the keeper speak to you during that first visit?" he asked.

"No."

The old man started, blinked in puzzlement. He mumbled to himself. "Strange . . . eliminates hypnosis . . . latent force in the statue . . . never took that rot about demonology seriously."

He checked himself hastily, and his glance met Bertrand's once again. He spoke very slowly.

"Then it was—*she*—who drew you back?"

There was that in his voice which caused Bertrand to affirm the truth, caused him to pour out his story in a ceaseless rush of words untouched by any attempt at concealment or adornment of the queer tale. At its conclusion, the old man sighed, heavily. He stared at the floor for a long time.

"I thought as much, my boy," Colonel Bertroux said. "Your family sent me down suspecting that something—or rather, someone, was holding you here. I had guessed that it was a woman, but I never dreamed that she was a woman of wax. But when you took me to the museum and I saw how you gazed at that statue, I knew. After looking at the image myself, I knew and understood far more. And then I heard the tale of the museum keeper. It started me thinking—if think I could, with a mind bemused by that damnable beauty of the cursed figure.

"At first, when I bid you good-bye, I intended to go. Not so much for your sake as for my own. Yes, I shall admit it frankly, I feared for myself. Bertrand, you understand the power that queer image holds over you, and other men as well, if the keeper is to be believed. That power it exercised upon me. I was frightened by the feeling I, an old man long forsaken by thoughts of love, experienced on seeing that red witch."

Bertrand stared at the colonel, who continued without heed.

"But I did not go back. The next day I returned to the museum in the morning, to gaze as you gazed, alone. And after an hour before that strange simulacrum, I left in a daze of wonder commingled with practical alarm. Whatever power that statue possessed, it was not good, or right, or wholly fashioned by sanity.

"I acted on impulse. I recalled the story of the museum keeper, this man Jacquelin. I went down to the newspaper offices to search the files. At last I found the case.

"Jacquelin had stated that the affair occurred many years ago, but he had not said just how many. My dear boy, that case was closed *over thirty years ago!*"

Bertrand's gasp was cut short as Bertroux rushed on.

"It was true, all true. There was a murder, and the wife of Doctor Jacquelin was convicted of it. It did come out that she had perpetrated five similar crimes under various names, and the journals of the day made capital out of certain testimony that was formally disbarred. This testimony spoke of wizardry and hinted that Madame Jacqueline was a witch, whose mad butcherings were actuated by a sort of sacrificial frenzy. The cult of the ancient goddess Hecate was mentioned, and the prosecution hinted that the red-headed woman was a priestess of some sort whose deeds constituted a monstrous worship. This offering of male blood in honor of a half-forgotten pagan deity was, naturally, disallowed as testimony; but there was enough evidence to convict the woman of the actual killings.

"It was fact, remember. And I uncovered things in the old papers of which this Jacquelin did not speak. The witchcraft theory was not formally recognized, but it got the doctor himself banned from the practice of medicine. It was more than substantiated that he was beginning to indulge in certain practices, encouraged by his wife: little pilferings of blood and flesh and sometimes vital organs from corpses in the morgues. That seems to be the real reason why he abandoned his practice after the trial and execution.

"The narrative about obtaining his wife's body from the morgue for sculpturing purposes is not mentioned, but there *is* an item about the body being *stolen*. And Jacquelin left Paris after the execution, thirty-seven years ago!"

The colonel's voice was harsh.

"You can imagine what this discovery did to me. I searched through year after year in the files, trying to trace the path of the man. Never did I find the name of Jacquelin mentioned. But occasionally little disturbing items about traveling waxworks exhibits cropped up. There was a wagon show run under the name of *Pallidi* which toured the Basque provinces in 1916. After it left one town, the bodies of two young men were discovered buried beneath the lot where the exhibition tent had been pitched. They were headless.

"A *George Balto* operated for a time in Antwerp under almost identical conditions about '24. He was called in to testify concerning the case of a mutilated body found in the streets outside his museum one morning, but was exonerated. There are other couplings of disappearance connected with waxworks, but the names and dates vary. In two of the later ones, however, the press reports distinctly describe a 'short, gray-haired proprietor.'

"What does it all mean? I wondered. My first impulse was to communicate with the *Sûreté,* but a pause convinced me that wild theories do not concern the police. There was much to be learned. The real mystery was just why men continue to stare at that statue. What is its power? I cast about for an explanation; for a time I guessed that the proprietor might be hypnotizing his solitary male visitors, using the statue as a medium. But why? For what purpose? And neither you nor myself was so hypnotized. No, there's something about that image alone; some secret power connected with it that smacks of—I must admit it—sorcery. She's like one of those ancient lamias one reads about in fairytales. One can't escape her.

"I couldn't. After leaving the newspaper offices that afternoon, I went back. I told myself that I was going to interview the little gray man, clear up the mystery. But in my heart I knew better. I brushed him aside as I entered the place and sought the statue. Once again I stared into her face and that terrible fascination of evil beauty flooded me. I tried to read her secret, but she read mine. I felt that she knew my emotion toward her, and that she rejoiced and exercised her cold power to rule my mind.

"I left in a daze. That evening at the hotel, while I tried to reason things out, to plan a course of action, I felt a strange urge to go back. It cut across my thoughts, and before I knew it, I was on the street, walking toward the museum. It was dark, and I returned home. The longing persisted. Before I could sleep, I was forced to bolt my door."

The colonel turned a sober face to Bertrand as he whispered.

"You, my friend, went to her willingly every day. Your torment at her aloofness was slight compared to mine, which fought against her enchantment. Because I would not go willingly, she compelled. Her anguishing memory haunted me. This morning, as I started here to see you, she forced my footsteps to the museum. That's why men go there—if willing, like you, they worship unbidden. If unwilling, she commands and they come. I went today. When you came, I was ashamed and left. Then I came here, to wait, and opened your door so that I might lock it from the inside and fight to keep from leaving until I could see you. I had to tell you this so that we might act together."

"What do you propose?" Bertrand asked. It was strange how earnestly he believed the other's story; he could realize only too easily that his beloved was evil without ceasing to adore her. He knew that he must fight against her siren magic even while his heart cried out to her. The colonel, he understood, shared his own feelings. Therefore he asked eagerly.

"We will go to the museum tomorrow," the colonel said. "Together we will be strong enough to fight against that power, suggestion—whatever it is. We can speak frankly to Jacquelin, hear him out. If he refuses to talk, we shall go to the police. I am convinced that there is something unnatural about all this; murder, hypnotism, magic, or just plain imagination, we must get to the bottom of it quickly. I fear for you, and for myself. That cursed statue is chaining me to the spot, and always it seeks to draw me back. Let us clear up this affair tomorrow, before it is too late."

"Yes," Bertrand agreed dully.

"Good. I will come for you about one in the afternoon. You will be ready?"

Bowing at Bertrand's nod of assent, the colonel withdrew.

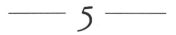

5

The poet worked all that evening on his poem; first to forget the strange tale of Bertroux, and second because he felt that he could not rest until he had completed his epic. In the back of his mind was a puzzling suspicion that he must work fast, that matters were coming to a head in such a fashion as to demand haste.

He was exhausted by daybreak, and somehow thankful that his tired sleep would be dreamless. He wanted to be free of that flame-haired image that haunted him by night, free to forget his terrible bondage to a wax woman.

He slept deeply as the sun crept from window to window of his attic room. When he arose, it was with the prescience that

noontide had passed, though by this time the sunlight had gradually faded into a mist of yellow fog that grew ever thicker
beyond the window-panes.

Glancing at his watch, he was startled to note that it was
already long past three o'clock.

Where was the colonel? Bertrand was confident that his con-
cierge would have awakened him with racket to spare should
he have a daytime visitor. No, the colonel had not come. And
that meant only one thing. He had been called, lured. Bertrand
jumped up, raced to the door.

Hastily he crammed the finished manuscript of his poem into
the ulster he donned against the encroaching fog. He took the
stairs hastily, then rushed out along the dismal, fog-drowned
streets.

This was like that first day, a month ago. And still he was
running to the museum to keep his inevitable tryst with torment.

The very moment seemed to make him forgetful of his real
errand, the finding of the colonel. Instead he could think only
of *her* as he rushed through the gray fog to the gray room, the
gray man, and the scarlet glory of her hair. . . .

The building loomed out of the mounting mists ahead. He
hurried down the stairs, entered. The place was deserted, the
little doorkeeper gone. A strange surmise rose in Bertrand's
heart, but it receded before an irresistible urge to commune
once more with Salome.

The air was tense with a feeling of impending fury, as though
the crystallization of some cosmic dread were near. The murderers leered waxenly within as he paced down the hall. No
Bertroux.

Deserted in the darkness, he stood alone before her. Never
had she seemed so radiant as today. In the half light she wavered,
slitted eyes shining with wild invitation to forbidden rhapsodies.
Her lips hungered.

Bertrand leaned forward, staring into that inscrutable, agelessly evil face. Something about her knowing smile of appeasement caused him to glance down—to glance at the silver salver that held the head of John the Baptist. Staring, still, wide-eyed it gaped.

The head of *Colonel Bertroux!*

Then he knew as he glanced at the mocking smile of anguish, glanced at the blood flooding forth from the slashed neck. *Realistic art!* The first head a month ago, the second last week, and now the colonel, who felt the flooding desire to return. Young men forever coming to worship her beauty—newspaper accounts of decapitation tragedies. The beauty of a murderess unveiled in a deserted wax museum—she who had beheaded her lovers for witchery. *How often was that head changed?*

The little gray man crouched at his back, his eyes filled with leaden fire. His hand held a surgeon's knife. He smiled—at her, and he mumbled.

"Why not? You love her. I love her. She was not like a mortal woman—she was a witch. Yes, she killed when she lived, she liked the blood of men and the sight of eyes forever fixed in worship of her beauty. We worshipped together her mistress Hecate. Then they guillotined her. And so—I stole the body to model this image. I became her priest. Men come and they desire her, and to them I bring the gift I bring to you. Because they love her, I give them what I can—the chance to rest their tortured heads within her hands. Wax hands, perhaps, but her spirit is near. They all feel her spirit, and that is why they come and adore. Her spirit talks to me at night and asks me to bring new lovers. We have traveled together many years, she and I, and now we have returned to Paris for new adorers. They must lie in her hands, bleeding and bright, and stare their stare of love forever into her face. When she tires, I give her a new admirer.

"The colonel came this morning, and when I told him that which I tell you, he consented. They all do. And you shall consent, my friend; I know you will. Think of it: to lie within her pale white hands and stare forever; to die with the benediction of her beauty in your eyes! You will make the sacrifice, won't you? No one will know; they never suspect. You will play John the Baptist? You want me to, now, don't you? You *want* me to—"

Hypnosis. Hypnosis at the last. Bertrand tried to move as the voice droned, the eyes stared in glorious pleading from above.

And the cold edge of the knife caressed his throat. The blade began to bite. He heard words through the gray fog, through the scarlet fog, as he stared into *her* face. She was a witch, a Medusa—to lie within her arms and worship as others had worshipped! A poet's death? In a moment his head would be resting on the salver and he could see her as he sank into the dark. He could never possess her—why live on? Why not die and know her radiance forever? It was easy, her husband knew, and he was being kind to Bertrand. Kind. The knife bit.

Bertrand's hand went up. A sudden horror flickered in his soul. He grappled with the screaming little madman, and the blade clattered to the floor. They fell in a lashing embrace, as Bertrand tore at the pudgy gray face, clawed deeply at the blazing eyes.

Something deep within him had risen in resurrection. Youth— sanity—the will to live. His fingers pressed as he shoved the gray man's head against the floor. He squeezed, throttled, until time dissolved in the welter of red anger. When his hands finally loosened, the little maniac lay quite still and dead.

Bertrand rose and faced his impassive goddess. Her smile

was unchanged. He looked again into her infernal beauty, and his soul wavered once more. Then his hands fumbled at the breast of his ulster and he gained courage.

He drew forth the crumpled manuscript that lay there—his finished poem to Salome.

He found matches.

He lit the manuscript. It flamed as he held it forth, held it to her flaming hair. Fire mingled with fire as she continued to stare in the way Bertrand could not yet understand, the terrible way that enchanted him and all men and lured them to their doom.

Impulse seized him even at the last. He took Salome in his arms—took her in his arms as she burned, writhing and moving with fiery life. He held her close for a moment as the glowing flames spread, then eased her again to the stand. She was burning horribly fast.

Witches must burn. . . .

And like a witch, her dying features changed. They melted into a hideous mass—her face became a gargoyle horror, a melting, shapeless yellow blob from which two glassy eyes fell like blue tears. Her body wiggled in agony as wax limbs sloughed. She was real then—real, and tortured. Tortured, just as Bertrand was as he beheld her waxen agonies. Tortured by fire, but a fire that purified.

Then it was all over. Bertrand stared at the man on the floor; still and dead he lay as the fire began creeping redly against the fog. It would soon blot the museum out forever, blot out the horror that lured men to a tragic re-enactment of an ancient crime. Fire purified.

Bertrand stared again at the little pile of melted yellow liquid that lay bubbling and seething as though in some hasty process of putrefaction. He stared, and then he prayed that the fire would mount swiftly. For now, with a gasp of horror, he understood, he knew the mystery of her allure which had eluded him.

The maniac murderer on the floor—he had fashioned the statue from the morgue-procured body of his wife. This he had told Bertrand. But now Bertrand saw more; he knew and guessed the secret of the statue's evil power. There is a miasma of evil about the dead body of a witch. . . .

Bertrand turned and ran sobbing from the redly ravaged room, ran sobbing from the sight of that yellow, bubbling pile of melted wax from which protruded the *charred, bony skeleton of a woman that had served as the statue's frame.*

MURDER AND
LONELY HEARTS

HELEN NIELSEN

HERBERT GIBSON WAS the last man who would have been suspected of wanting to kill his wife. He was the prototype of the
good citizen: He belonged to the local Chamber of Commerce,
two service organizations, the Athletic Club—which he hadn't visited in ten years and thirty pounds—and attended church every
Easter, Christmas, and Mother's Day. The latter was a concession
to Irene (Mrs. Gibson) who, in their twenty-six years of marriage,
had mothered three cocker spaniels and a French poodle.

On the surface, the Gibson marriage was a happy one. None of
their neighbors on Acacia Lane, that suburban paradise for the
middle income group, could say anything against them. They were
a quiet, conservative couple in their mid-forties, who kept their
house painted, their two Chevrolets polished, and their lawns clipped
and green, which was a matter of great significance on Acacia Lane.
Residents of long tenure might have noted, had their memories
been equally green, that Herbert Gibson had worn a somewhat
bitter expression when he began walking the earliest cocker span-

iel; but with succeeding years and successive cocker spaniels this expression had gradually altered to resignation, benign resignation and finally, by the time Irene switched to the poodle, a kind of absentminded serenity which, in the latter months, approached nirvana.

There was, however, nothing absentminded about the manner in which Herbert conducted his business. He was a C.P.A.—twenty-five years in the same location: Room 408 Handley Building. It was an old building. The offices were small, dingy, but inexpensive, and Herbert saw no object in providing luxurious surroundings merely for the purpose of telling clients how much they owed the government. Irene, who wasn't interested in business, was vaguely aware that he went off somewhere or other every day to do something or other, for which he received a fairly adequate income.

Herbert wasn't ambitious. If he occasionally felt a vague stirring or uneasiness within, he stopped off at the drugstore for a bicarbonate and forgot about it. But that was before Rodney Dumbarton, Business Management, moved into the adjoining office. Whatever business Dumbarton managed was none of Herbert's— they met only on occasions when the postman erred as to his choice of mail slots—until the day his neighbor departed mere minutes ahead of the police. It developed that Mr. Dumbarton had managed to collect substantial sums of money from clients for services never rendered, a practice considered antisocial in law enforcement circles.

The fact that he'd been in contact with an absconded criminal was one of the most exciting things that had ever happened to Herbert. He tried to share the experience with Irene at dinner, but anything pertaining to his business bored Irene. All he had to say was "An interesting thing happened at the office today," and her face, never really attentive, took on an expression of complete remoteness. She stirred her asparagus with a fork and stared over the top of Herbert's slightly balding head.

"I'm getting awfully tired of that Currier and Ives over the mantel," she remarked.

Herbert tried again.

"Mr. Dumbarton, next door to me, left just ahead of the police. He was mixed up in the darndest—"

"I think it's the snow I dislike," Irene added. "It's so cold-looking."

"—scheme," Herbert said. "He'd distributed a lot of phoney advertising for something called a 'Friendship Cruise.' Here, I brought one of his brochures home with me."

Irene paid no more heed to the brochure than she had to Herbert.

"The room needs more color."

"His idea was to get unmarried men and women corresponding with one another through his office and then sell them passage on one of his cruises. It was a sort of floating lonely hearts club."

Herbert paused, smiling at his own feeble attempt at humor. Finally, Irene did look at him.

"Herbert," she said, "eat your lamb chop. Celeste is waiting for the bone. She's been very patient."

Herbert sighed and put the brochure down on the table. The conversation had gone the way of all their conversations: Irene hadn't heard a word he'd said.

With no one to talk to, Herbert soon forgot about Rodney Dumbarton and his extravagant scheme until one morning a week later when he was going through the morning mail and came across the following letter:

Friendship Cruises, Inc.

Dear Sir:
I am writing in response to your interesting brochure only because you sound as if you are a highly respectable organization and would have a highly respectable clientele. . . .

At this point Herbert realized the postman had erred again, and that he had compounded the postman's error with his letter opener; but two typewritten sheets remained, and curiosity got the better of virtue. He continued:

> . . . *This is very important to me as I am a respectable lady, over thirty, who has never traveled abroad, and the idea of getting acquainted with someone on shipboard before sailing seems wonderful.*
>
> *You suggest a brief autobiography and information on my likes and dislikes. There really isn't much to tell about me. I make my living from tax accounting; but I would prefer companionship with someone in some other kind of work, preferably a writer or an artist, but most of all someone who is an interesting conversationalist. I would love to have someone to talk to.*
>
> *It is difficult to say what I like to do, because I've never had time to do it and find out. I can only tell you what I've always dreamed of doing if I ever went abroad. Most of all, I want to go to Paris. I want to visit the Louvre and see the famous paintings, and visit Notre Dame cathedral and see the Rose Window, and sit at one of those little tables outside a sidewalk cafe and have whatever people have at sidewalk cafes. I even want to take the elevator to the top of the Eiffel Tower!*
>
> *I suppose I sound just like the typical tourist, but I will be waiting to hear from any of your clients whom you think might be interested in knowing me.*
>
> *Respectfully,*
>
> *Sylvia Sagan*
> *Box 1477, City*
>
> *P.S. I am a blonde with hazel eyes and have what my friends tell me is a good figure.*

What had started as curiosity blossomed into astonishment by the time Herbert finished reading the letter. Was there such a woman as Sylvia Sagan? *I would love to have somebody to talk to.* The words had a poignant quality that aroused Herbert's sympathy. *It's difficult to say what I'd like to do because I've never had time to find out.* At this point the writer placed a mirror to Herbert's soul. He raised his eyes. The door to his office stood open. The gold lettering, chipped with the passing years, told him his identity: Herbert Gibson, Certified Public Accountant. Somewhere in the city was another office: Sylvia Sagan, Tax Accountant. It might even be very much like his own—one desk, two chairs, a water cooler in the corner, and a calendar on the wall with a picture of puppies at play.

Herbert's eyes followed the direction of his thoughts and suddenly came to an arresting halt. The calendar didn't have a picture of puppies at play, Irene's perennial selection; it had a picture of a seacoast—and a wild one at that! And then he remembered why he'd done the choosing this year. There were two lines underneath the picture that had struck his fancy:

> *I must go down to the seas again,*
> *To the lonely sea and the sky—*

They were from a poem he'd memorized in high school English. He'd been darned good at English, come to think of it. He'd written several A compositions and tried his hand at a few short stories before he married Irene. *I would prefer companionship with someone in some other kind of work, preferably a writer.* . . . Herbert reined in his imagination and replaced the letter in an envelope. He would return it to the sender, of course, with a note of explanation the first time he had a few minutes to spare.

And that is exactly what he would have done, if Irene's brother Lennie hadn't been parked in his favorite chair in front of the television when he got home that night.

Lennie was a problem. He had won a Purple Heart in World War II and was still bleeding. He was getting a bit old to be a member of the Lost Generation, and anyhow, Lennie wasn't lost. He just didn't know what had become of everybody else. He did, however, know the way to Herbert's house whenever he was in need, and his unheralded appearance precipitated another fruitless conversation.

"I suppose Lennie's lost his job again," Herbert said to Irene irritably.

"You didn't even notice the new picture I bought for over the mantel," Irene said to Herbert.

"Or is his wound bothering him again—that knicked finger he got on the target range in Georgia?"

"I think the coloring is much nicer, don't you?"

"Hang it all, Irene, you know how he monopolizes the television, and this is my night for 'Foreign Escapade'!"

"It's a genuine reproduction of a genuine Matisse, Herbert. Just think, a genuine Matisse!"

Herbert took Celeste for a walk.

It was a foggy night, and he almost enjoyed walking Celeste on a foggy night. She was less conspicuous and so was Acacia Lane. The houses of the neighbors—the Meekers, the Swansons, Dr. Pettigrew—were just so many dim forms behind the mist; and with a little imagination the street could become the Limehouse District, or a coastal town in Normandy, or any other place where mystery stalked the shadows.

> *Who is Sylvia? What is she?*
> *That all her swains commend her? . . .*

He hadn't thought of those lines since he was courting Irene and they sang them together at her mother's upright. It seemed impossible now that they had ever done anything together. To Irene, he was just a man who walked the dog, while Lennie watched television. What kind of a man would he be, if he'd ever had time to do what he wanted to do? A letter began to write itself in his mind.

Dear Miss Sagan,
Your letter has been forwarded to me by Friendship Cruise.
I must say that it is a very interesting letter with certain
passages that lead me to believe we have much in common.
Oddly enough, we're in almost the same business—

No, the last sentence wouldn't do. Sylvia wanted to corre-
spond with someone in a different field, preferably a writer or
an artist. Herbert made a mental erasure.

Oddly enough, in view of your request, I am a writer of
short stories. Not a very successful one, I'm afraid; but
then, like yourself, I've never had anyone I could really
talk to or have share my dreams. That's important, don't
you think? To know someone who cares about what you
are doing—who believes in you and wants to be a part
of your life?
   Your ideas on travel are charming, Miss Sagan; but
not nearly as charming, I'm sure, as you must be. I hope
you will honor me by acknowledging this letter and tell-
ing me more about yourself.
                              Respectfully yours—

Herbert Gibson didn't sound proper at the end of the letter
any more than the letter sounded like Herbert Gibson. It was
more in the style of Rodney Dumbarton's romantic brochure.
His name hadn't appeared anywhere on the piece—still, he
wanted something crisper.

                    Respectfully yours,
                    Rodney Barton

That was better. Celeste stopped and Herbert stopped. A
shapely blonde emerged out of the fog and walked past them.

Herbert stared, remembering a postscript and adding it to his own mental missile.

P.S. I am a little past forty. I have light brown hair, blue eyes, and work out regularly at the Athletic Club.

It was only a letter in his mind, but it was astonishing how much satisfaction it gave him. It wouldn't be fair to actually write it. Or would it? It wasn't as if there really were a cruise. What harm could one letter do? He might give the poor woman a bright day in her drab little office with the water cooler and the calendar on the wall. He wouldn't have to risk exposure by using his own address; he could take a post office box. . . .

The fog gave Herbert daring, but it was Lennie who gave him decision. He returned to the house just in time for "Foreign Escapade." Lennie was watching wrestling.

"My gosh, Herbie, what do you want with that kid stuff? Watch this now! Abdullah's got a sleeper hold on the Cowboy. Ride 'em Cowboy!"

Herbert unsnapped Celeste's leash and went upstairs. Irene was in her bedroom reading a novel. She didn't so much as look up when he came to the door.

"I just want to borrow your typewriter to write a letter," he said.

She didn't answer, naturally.

The correspondence between Rodney Barton and Sylvia Sagan began innocently enough. It was all very well to write one letter and then terminate the correspondence, but why just one letter? As long as nothing could come of it anyway, what harm could be done? Herbert needed some entertainment now that Lennie had settled down with the television.

And certain things demanded an answer.

*. . . I can tell by your letter, Mr. Barton, that you are
a very interesting person. You must meet fascinating
people in your work, and I'm flattered that you would
even think of writing to me. You've no idea how dull
my life is! How I, too, long for someone to share my
dreams!*

*Have you decided definitely on the cruise? I still want
to visit Paris, but there's also Rome. . . .*

*P.S. I'm enclosing a recent snapshot. It's not very good
but it will give you some idea of what I'm like.*

The snapshot wasn't very good—Sylvia was too far from the
camera to give any distinct features to her face. But it had been
taken on a beach, and although the bathing suit might have been
a little out of fashion—Herbert wasn't an expert on such matters—the contents were arranged in a quite satisfactory way.
This troubled him. He'd written to her only out of the kindness
of his heart to give the poor woman something to dream on a
bit longer. Why was her life so dull? And then he read the letter
again . . . "you are a very interesting person . . ." Perhaps that
was true. Perhaps all he needed was for someone to hold up
the mirror and let him see himself for what he could be. That
might be the case with Sylvia, too. There could be no harm in
one more letter.

Dear Miss Sagan,
*Do you really imagine that my life is exciting, or that
I have met anyone more interesting than you? Your
letters are like a breath of fresh air on a stifling day.
What a marvelous thing to have found a woman who
is interesting and interested in others.*

*It would be criminal to go abroad and not visit the
Eternal City. I would love to be able to escort you through
the galleries, the cathedrals and the old ruins.*

[59]

Incidentally, have you ever been married? I ask only because your snapshot makes it seem incredible that you were not.

Cordially,
Rodney

P.S. May I call you Sylvia?

The postscript was accidental; it seemed to write itself. This wasn't turning out at all the way Herbert intended. He had the vague sensation of being sucked into a whirlpool, but he mailed the letter anyway.

Dear Rodney,
You're right, we must be honest with one another. Yes, I have been married—unhappily. I hope you won't be angry with me for not having told you of this sooner; but I did want to make your acquaintance, and was afraid you would think me forward. After all, the past is the past, don't you agree? When two people have so much in common, they should enjoy one another and no questions asked.
Have you thought of Spain?

Dearest Sylvia,
I think of nothing but Spain—and you! But now I, too, must make a confession. It was only by accident that I opened your first letter. You see, I work in an office adjoining Friendship Cruises and received it by mistake when the company went out of business several weeks ago. I meant only to return your letter with an explanation of why it had been opened, but you sounded like someone I wanted to know. I realize that I shouldn't have continued this long without telling you the truth, but I hope we are close enough friends now that you can forgive.

There are no Friendship Cruises, Sylvia dear, but there are still friendships that sometimes become life voyages. We can escape the humdrum world. Fortunately, I have a little property. . . .

It was madness. Even as he posted the letter, Herbert knew that Irene would never consent to a divorce, and even if she did, they would have to divide the property. The house was clear and would realize a nice profit, but half of that profit, less court fees . . . and he might not even get half if Irene learned about Sylvia! No, it was stark madness. It was what happened to a man after having his wife's brother planted in front of the television for six weeks. But he couldn't put all the blame on Lennie. There was still that stormy seascape on the calendar— the omen. And now everything hinged on Sylvia's answer. Perhaps she wouldn't answer. The thought came with both pain and relief, for even then Herbert knew what he really had in mind.

Sylvia did answer.

Rod, my dearest,
How can I be so lucky? Or was it only luck? Do you believe in fate? Now I can tell you how timid I was about writing to Friendship Cruises. Their brochure made everything sound so wonderful, and I was simply dying of loneliness; but I was afraid of the type of person who might answer their offer. Now I don't have to be afraid because you weren't even a client. I suppose it's cruel of me, but I'm really happy the company went out of business.

You write that you have a little property you could dispose of. So have I. It may take a few weeks to liquidate my holdings, but I've waited a lifetime. A few weeks longer won't kill me. . . .

The language of Sylvia's letter was almost brutal. What had started as an innocent prank, had reached an irrevocable conclusion: Irene had to go.

But how? Herbert had never contemplated murder—in spite of Lennie's visits. How many means were there? Irene looked at him suspiciously when she found him tampering with the kitchen window. And he decided a faked robbery and shooting wouldn't work anyway. Irene was annoyed when he managed to bump into her a few times at the head of the stairs. That sort of thing was much too risky, really. The fall might not kill her. He'd be in a worse position than ever then, with an invalid on his hands. The axe in the garage was out of the question. Herbert always felt nauseous at the sight of blood.

The solution, unexpectedly, came from Irene herself.

"The rosebushes are getting a blight," she remarked over the breakfast table.

Herbert was deep in his problem.

"You're putting on a little weight, Irene," he said. "Why don't you do something for exercise—horseback riding, for instance?"

"Horseback?" It was the first time she'd heard him in years. "You know I'm terrified of horses. I was thrown when I was a girl."

"I know, but I don't think you should go through life being afraid of anything. I'll go with you."

Irene stared at him strangely. She'd been staring at him strangely ever since the window episode.

"I am afraid of nothing," she said firmly, "except the blight on the roses. Are you listening to me, Herbert? I want you to stop off and buy some arsenic—"

Herbert was listening.

"—and while you're about it, pick up a bottle of wine for dinner. It's Lennie's birthday."

"Wine?" Herbert echoed.

Irene's voice softened.

"I know it's an extravagance, Herbert. But I want the dinner to be something special. I didn't tell you before, but Lennie's leaving soon. This may be the last time we're all together on his birthday."

Irene had become a prophetess.

Arsenic and wine—the classic means of murder. There was still a matter of mechanics to work out. But when the Fates were with you, what could go wrong? Herbert sat in his office and listened to the surf pounding on the rocky shore in the calendar picture—the omen. Now he understood what had been happening to him when he chose that calendar—happening long before he'd heard of Friendship Cruises or gone walking Celeste in the fog. Sylvia had only roused the dormant senses; he really *was* Rodney Barton—always had been. He had only been slumbering all through the years and now he was awakening.

And Rodney Barton could do anything. Arsenic and wine . . . he needed a small container. He left his office and walked down a flight to the dentist in 304. He complained of a toothache he didn't have, and then returned to his own office with a small bottle of oil of cloves which he promptly dumped down the drain. The small bottle was what he needed.

At noon, Herbert went out for lunch and stopped at the gardening shop where he'd traded for years. They made up a special arsenic solution of their own that came bottled, boxed, wrapped in paper and sealed with a strip of gummed advertising tape. The tape was never very tight. As soon as he left the shop, Herbert peeled off the strip being careful not to tear it, and returned to his office. There he managed to unwrap the bottle without damaging the paper or the box and—careful not to get his fingerprints on the bottle—transferred a small portion of the contents into the empty oil of cloves bottle. That done, he rewrapped the bottle, retaped the seal—with the aid of the office mucilage—and surveyed his work with smug satisfaction.

[63]

He knew Irene. She opened every package the moment it was placed in her hands; only her fingerprints would be on the arsenic.

He envisioned himself, shocked and grief-stricken, telling the police how Irene had asked him to buy the arsenic and the wine, and he, in all innocence, had done so without realizing the dark significance of her parting words: "This may be the last time we're all together."

Suicide was much more tragic than an accident. The neighbors would see nothing strange in a quick sale of the property so he could get away from bitter memories—away to Spain, warm and exciting with dark-eyed beauties dancing in the sunlight, and Sylvia, of course. Sylvia who really understood him—and if it turned out that she didn't, there were always the dark-eyed beauties. Herbert leaned back in his chair, and for the first time in his life, put his feet up on the desk. He was going to enjoy being Rodney Barton.

On birthdays, holidays, and festive occasions, Irene used candles on the table. Herbert counted on that and wasn't disappointed. For contemplated sleight of hand, the less light the better. He didn't open the wine bottle. Lennie was more proficient at that art, and the search for a corkscrew took him safely off to the kitchen. Irene—to whom Herbert had given the arsenic, and who ripped the covering from the bottle in order to make certain he hadn't made a stupid mistake and bought the wrong preparation—was busy with her dinner. There was plenty of time during one of her absences from the room to transfer a few drops of poison from the small bottle in his pocket to the wine glass in front of her plate. It was a colorless liquid—not noticeable in the candlelight.

It was done. Herbert replaced the bottle in his pocket and stepped back from the table. Strange how he could hear that surf on the rocks again—louder than it had been before. It was actually done. It wasn't something lurking in the back of his mind as he typed out mad letters to Sylvia. And they were mad letters. He realized that now with a sudden, sharp clarity that came like a lifting of the fog. Who was Sylvia? Who was she to make Herbert Gibson a murderer? No, not Herbert. It was Rodney who had done it—Rodney Barton.

"Herbert—Herbert, do sit down. We're waiting for you."

Herbert looked up, startled. He hadn't even heard Irene and Lennie come into the room, and there they were seated at the table ready to begin dinner. Lennie was pouring the wine.

"Wait, Lennie—" Irene said. "I think there's something *in* this glass."

He saw her hand reach out—but to his glass, not to hers.

"Dust," she said. "I was sure that I washed out those glasses."

Irene left the table, glass in hand, and in a moment there was the sound of the faucet running in the kitchen. And it was then Herbert became aware of a terrible loss: Rodney Barton was gone! He couldn't go through with it; he simply didn't have the nerve. But Lennie was still pouring wine. Irene's glass was full—blood-red and full. He had to get that glass somehow; but she returned too soon. Lennie filled Herbert's glass. It was time for the toast. Herbert's hand was trembling as he reached forward. If there was nothing short of snatching the poisoned drink from Irene's hand, he'd have to do just that. And then he thought of a way.

"Celeste," he said sharply. "Where's Celeste? We have to get the whole family in on this."

When Celeste bounded up to the table, there was a momentary distraction, one just long enough for Herbert to switch glasses with Irene. They could proceed with the festivities then—Herbert so shaken from his brush with homicide, he nearly forgot himself and drank along with the others. Just in time, he realized what he was doing and made a splendid job of spilling the contents of his glass all over the damask cloth.

"Herbert, what have you done?"

The voice of a shrew, but music to his ears. Irene's glass was empty and she could still berate him.

"You've spilled your wine, you clumsy fool! You've spilled it all!"

Sheer music. Herbert made his way to the kitchen for a towel, and Irene's chosen phrases followed him all the way. He didn't care. She could scold for the rest of their days just as long as he could hear her voice. And then it stopped. He listened, but the voice didn't come again—only the *thud*.

When Dr. Pettigrew and the policeman came down the stairs, Herbert was sitting in his chair with his face buried in his hands. He pulled the hands away slowly and looked up at them with haggard eyes. Lennie was with them, too, standing a few steps behind. He held something in his hands.

"I don't know what happened," Herbert said vaguely. "I just don't know—"

"It was arsenic poisoning," the policeman said. "One sniff of the glass was enough to convince me, and the doctor agrees. Your wife died of arsenic poisoning."

"But she couldn't have! I spilled—"

Dr. Pettigrew stepped forward and placed a restraining hand on his shoulder.

"Take it easy, Mr. Gibson. I know how you feel. This is incredible to me, too. Why, I've known you and Irene for years. I was just telling the sergeant, here, that I couldn't imagine what could get into a woman to do what she did."

"What *she* did?"

Pettigrew's face was grave.

"You've got to brace yourself, Herbert. Irene put the arsenic in the wine. We know that because Lennie tells us she'd been after him for days to buy it, but he never got around to it. I suppose she thought she could count on her own brother to cover for her. And tonight at the table, she found an excuse to take your glass out to the kitchen, didn't she? And when you spilled your wine, she was terribly upset, wasn't she? Don't you see, Herbert? Somehow or another Irene made a mistake with the glasses, but the poisoned drink was meant for you."

"For me?" Herbert echoed. "But why—"

Three faces looked at him with varying degrees of pity, and then Lennie handed him a package of letters.

"We found these in Irene's room," he said. "Read them and you'll know why."

But Herbert didn't have to read the letters. The address was sufficient: Sylvia Sagan. Box 1477, City.

"Mr. Gibson! Mr. Gibson! are you all right?"

Herbert looked up with the eyes of a small boy trying to comprehend. Celeste, the French poodle, the Matisse over the mantel, the brochure he'd left on the dining table. Slowly, he understood.

"She wanted someone to talk to," he said.

THE TSANTSA

MAURICE SANDOZ

FOR THE BENEFIT of those of my readers who do not know the meaning of the word *tsantsa*—and there is nothing they need to be ashamed of in that—I will start with a definition.

It is Indian in origin and is still only familiar to the Jivaros Indian tribes dwelling on the equator in districts where very few Europeans have ever been. It denotes a singular war trophy: the head of an enemy who has been decapitated but not scalped. Processes which have remained more or less secret, have not merely rendered these heads immune from decay, they have so much reduced their proportions that their size varies from that of an orange to that of a duck's egg. The strange thing is that this shrinking, this contraction of the tissues, does not involve any deformation of the victim's features. His face remains perfectly recognizable; only the scale of it is different. Shall we say, we seem to be looking at it "through the wrong end of the telescope"; that is all.

If we are to believe the theories that have been advanced by explorers about the preparation of these grim trophies, this is what they give us as the approved recipe. But I fear it may discourage my readers, especially those of the fair sex, even more than the recipe of the great Vatel, who, when describing the method of roasting a chicken, began with these words: "Take the gravy of three fine ducks. . . ."

Here, then, is the recipe of the explorers:

Take the head of your enemy without plucking the hair off; see that it has been recently separated from the trunk. With the help of a very sharp instrument—scissors for cutting up game will do admirably—incise the scalp right around, starting from the dint in the nape of the neck. It is important to see that the line of incision leaves the hair untouched and stops at the forehead just where the hair begins to grow. Doing it this way makes it easier to conceal the incision.

Working with a gentle and at the same time firm touch, which you will easily acquire at your third or fourth head, open the two tips of the incision you have made and gradually peel off the whole of the skin from the skull and all the muscles of the face, taking great care that nothing should be torn.

Inside this limp mask place a round stone the dimensions of which should be slightly smaller than those of the head of your enemy. This stone should be of the temperature of boiling oil, which is what you will have used to heat it with.

Sew up the wound, moisten the face with fermented fruit juice—a wine lends itself perfectly to this ablution—in which you have left pomegranate peel to soak, or the skin of any other fruit that is rich in tannin, and expose your handiwork to the rays of the sun for eight hours, keeping away the flies, which will try to make for so attractive a morsel.

Next day, take out the stitches and replace the

stone by another hot one, exactly like the first except that it should be slightly smaller in size.

By repeating this operation every day until the shrunk tissues refuse to contract any farther, you will at last have obtained the head of which you have dreamed and will be able to enjoy the reward of your efforts.

In order to prevent the results of so much trouble from being spoiled, it will be as well to insert a lump of camphor in the mouth of the tsantsa before, of course, proceeding to the first operation, because at a later stage the lips, which incidentally should be sewn up with gut, harden and cannot be parted again.

By acting on these instructions you stand more chance of preserving your tsantsa for the delight of generations to come.

It was at Marseilles that, thanks to the good offices of Dr. Marchand, I paid my first visit to a lunatic asylum. The strange thing is that during this very first visit I happened straight away to meet with one of the most curious cases of insanity it has ever been my lot to study, like the person who has never in his life touched a card yet sometimes breaks the bank at Monte Carlo.

I ought perhaps to say that, though my first easy success encouraged me to persevere, I needed a deal of patience to find others to serve as worthy pendants to it.

The private nursing home in Marseilles was not far from the zoological gardens, and I at once got a queer impression from visiting patients who lived behind locked doors, when I had just been watching the animals imprisoned behind the solid bars of their cages.

Dr. Marchand, with whom I was perfectly frank about the object of my visit, looked me up and down with a thoughtful, rather surly expression. Suddenly his face brightened.

"I've got it," he cried in a tone of relief. "As you may well imagine, I am bounded by the rules of professional secrecy. Most of my patients belong to good and"—here the doctor hesitated a moment—"well-to-do families of the town and neighborhood. The less talk there is about them, the better pleased these relations are with me.

"Anyway, among my guests is a man of about forty who does not come from these parts but has a family living in Brazil. The family defrays the cost of his maintenance once a year by check—payment, I need hardly say, being made in advance. They never inquire after his health, for which I don't blame them as he is incurable, except to ask whether José F. is still alive and whether they are bound in consequence to continue paying for his keep.

"My impression is that if I talk to you of this man and his case, I am not likely to injure the patient or his relatives.

"Do you care to follow me?"

I acquiesced and followed Dr. Marchand up to the second story, a relatively new part of the building, where those who are convalescent and tired are supposed to "rest"; persons who, for the most part, will never see Marseilles again except through the barred windows of their rooms, which, I may add, are clean and comfortable.

Dr. Marchand knocked at the door of a room which was situated, as I still recall, at the corner of the corridor. A deep voice answered, "Come in."

Stretched at length on an easy chair, muffled in a shawl and wearing only a dressing gown, was a man with strong features and still young in years.

What struck me first of all about him was the elegance of his hands: the hands, I thought, of a mummy, they were so long and emaciated.

Next, it was his face which held my attention. I could hardly take my eyes from it.

The features were regular, the brows beautifully shaped above handsome, bright eyes; the bow of the lips too was very regular and sensual. And yet I derived no pleasure from looking at his face.

There must have been something missing somewhere. I soon found out what it was when the man rose to greet us.

He was tall and, at the first glance, seemed well proportioned, but the head was not in scale with the rest. If it did not spoil his appearance when he was seen in profile, as soon as he looked at you full face you perceived that it was too small to crown the body adequately. I compared it in my mind to the pommel of a riding whip. The forehead, without actually retracting, had something "squeezed" about it, which left a disagreeable impression.

The last of his race, I thought, and sat down.

I had time to look around me while the doctor was asking after the health of his patient.

There were books—lots of books, in different languages. The complete works of Proust kept company with those of Thomas Mann, volumes of Lawrence and Huxley with those of D'Annunzio.

The perfect order in which the room was kept gave no hint that the mind of its occupant was wandering.

"My friend would like to make your acquaintance," the doctor said to him, after having come to the end of his usual questions. "He is studying metaphysical as well as physical problems. Thus I was led to talk about you. From motives of discretion I did not allude to the matter, but if you felt disposed to submit your case to him exactly as you did to me on your arrival in Marseilles, I fancy you would interest him enormously and would also be of assistance to anyone—should there ever be anyone— who might be tempted to repeat your dangerous experiment."

I must confess that the doctor's preamble excited my curiosity to the highest pitch, and in my mind I put up a prayer that the patient might not seek refuge in an obstinate silence. Psychiatrists will bear me out that this is what happens only too often.

"My experiment!" exclaimed José F. "My crime, is what you mean, Doctor. You have hit on the one argument to induce me to repeat, for the very last time, the narrative of the events which brought me to you."

Dr. Marchand got up.

"You are aware, Don José, that I know your story by heart. You never change the tenor of it or even the order of events. That being so, you will excuse me if I leave you alone with my friend. You know how many guests"—I noticed that the doctor avoided, so far as he could, using the word *patient*—"are asking for me every moment, and I must see that I don't make enemies of them."

"You go, Doctor. Your friend shall rejoin you as soon as he has heard it all. Please observe I do not say 'as soon as he has believed it all.' "

The doctor slipped away, but not till he had handed me a box of cigarettes. "You may need them," he said. "The story you are about to hear is not a short one."

"I need not introduce myself," my interlocutor began. "It is enough that you should know that I am French, and that I have no claim to the title 'Don José' bestowed on me by Dr. Marchand, who likes to have his little joke. My father was born in Brazil and made a fortune in the sugar industry. When he died he left his property to his brother, who is my guardian, or, rather, who became such when I entered this—boarding house. My mother died at my birth, and I was brought up at the College of the Immaculate Conception at Rio as soon as I was of an age to be admitted.

"I think—an ' the doctor shares my view—that it was this complete lack of any maternal tenderness, for which neither my contacts with indifferent schoolfellows nor my distant relationships with priests could possibly compensate, that was the reason for my being conscious, long before reaching the age of puberty, of a growing desire for feminine company. I will go even further and confess that it was a desire to be governed, taught and, above all, dominated by someone of the other sex who was gentle and at the same time self-willed."

I noticed that Don José stressed the word *self-willed* with special satisfaction.

Ha! thought I. A victim, no doubt, of masochism.

And Mr. F. continued his story:

"All the women I knew in Brazilian society seemed to me too gentle and submissive for me to be able to pick my ideal in them. Centuries of Portuguese influence and constant preoccupation with their religious observances have fitted them for all the duties, but also for all the sacrifices, that marriage demands. On the other hand, they are soon at a loss when faced by unforeseen difficulties. On a journey, for instance, they are terrified by everything: by unfamiliar food, by foreign languages—even by Spanish, in spite of its being closely allied to their mother tongue; the smallest thing upsets them, and everything frightens them—the sight of an unknown insect, for instance, or even dealing with servants they have not seen before.

"I quickly realized that I should never find in Rio, at any rate among Brazilians of the feminine sex, the young woman of energy"—Here again I noticed that the patient took a definite pleasure in pronouncing the word *energy*—"who was to rescue me from the circle of males in which from my earliest childhood I had too long been imprisoned. I was wary of masculine brutality with its vulgarity and its tendency to persecution."

(At the word *persecution*, I pricked up my ears. Was I about to listen to some confidences from a victim of persecution mania? That would have been particularly interesting for me; but I found I was mistaken.)

"Rio, as you well know, is a seaport where every year boats deposit batches of foreigners, who arrive from all parts of the world and often settle down there, in the hopes of making, or remaking, a fortune. Some have been attracted by the beauty of the capital, adorned with its fringe of beaches; others have come to study the range of the country's inexhaustible resources.

"It was just after the American liner *New Star* had berthed that I met Alice and her mother.

"They had come to Rio de Janeiro to collect the inheritance of a brother of Alice's. During his lifetime he had been regarded as an unsatisfactory subject whose negative qualities and positive defects had kept his kindred aloof from him. But as soon as the family discovered that he had left some property, they also discovered that he had possessed some merits, and brazenly proclaimed their relationship."

Here José F. broke off:

"The family I refer to," said he, "was pretty well known. Would you like me to call them . . . Hoyet?"

I made a gesture of acquiescence.

"The difficulties inseparable from unfreezing the funds kept Mrs. Hoyet and her daughter tied to Brazil, where they were able to live by nibbling at this unexpected capital. I fancy that Mrs. Hoyet's resources in New York were on the modest side and that the expedition to Brazil, which enabled them to carry on without touching their American income, must have struck her as providential. In any case, mother and daughter left their hotel and took rooms in Rio in one of the tiny colonial houses sheltering in the shadow of the skyscrapers that border the seashore at Copacabana."

While I listened to this narrative, which formed, in a way, the prologue to José F.'s adventures, I could not help reflecting that if his brain was disturbed, there were no signs whatsoever of any such disturbance in his talk, and I could not but admire the clearness of his exposition and applaud his logic and regard for chronology.

"Unless I am mistaken, I was introduced to Mrs. Hoyet at a charity bazaar. I made myself agreeable to her before I had seen the daughter, who was a famous beauty, and she appreciated this, perceiving that my gallantry was disinterested. I think she was rather exasperated at always being 'the mother of the beautiful Alice' and at having the still visible relics of her own beauty so often ignored.

"At her third glass of champagne, she decided that I was a 'nice boy' and introduced me to her daughter.

"I invited Alice to dance a tango. Ah, that tango! I still remember it."

(Good heavens, thought I, if he does not spare me a description of his first tango with Miss Hoyet, whenever shall we get to the main action?)

"Miss Hoyet danced admirably; but I noticed one rather curious thing, that although her movements were in harmony with mine she did not submit entirely to the will of her partner.

"Don't misunderstand me. There was never any question of actual resistance on her part; that would have upset our dancing. But, how shall I put it? It was a case of collaboration which was not entirely disinterested. Thus I became aware that while she simulated submission, it was she who 'guided' me, though I was hardly conscious of it.

"Locked together, we revolved under the chandeliers of the Casino ballroom, but we never drew near the corner of the room where Mrs. Hoyet, in hopeless solitude, was smoking cigarettes, leaning her elbows on the marble table behind which our empty chairs awaited us.

"I used all my ingenuity to compel my partner to approach the spot where her mother sat. Each time, without, as I said before, any apparent pressure on her part, she succeeded in making me avoid this part of the room, which called up in her mind, I imagine, some sort of constraint, or perhaps the supervision, however kind, of her liberty.

"Believe me, I was in heaven. I had at last met the woman

to 'dominate' me, which was the secret desire of my heart.

"As you may well imagine, things did not stop short at a tango. We saw each other day after day, and the two of us wandered about Rio and its delightful surroundings. We were often to be found under the trees of the famous botanical gardens. There, in the quiet of tropical arbors, I had time to observe and gradually to discover the strange character of my companion.

"She disliked beautiful things, but took an interest in what was curious—even in what was monstrous. She would pass by roses without giving them a glance and magnolias without enjoying their scent, but she stopped in front of the insect-eating plants, fascinated by them, though they are hideous, and stood for a long time gazing at the horrible Aristolochias and the rather frightening calyxes of the arums.

" 'Look at this flower,' she said. 'Isn't it like a spider? Like a spider which has just caught a butterfly! And this arum looks artificial, as though it had been made up out of a piece of snake skin.'

"That made me a little uncomfortable, certainly, but only a little! Youthful exuberance, thought I, and the fascination exercised by unusual shapes.

"We also visited the zoological gardens of Rio and wandered about admiring—at any rate I did—its marvelous collection of birds.

" 'We must come back again on Thursday,' Miss Hoyet finally said.

" 'Why Thursday?' I asked in surprise.

" 'It's on Thursday that they feed the snakes,' she calmly answered.

"We did in fact go back there on a Thursday, and even now I regret our visit. No one who has not seen a boa constrictor first strangle and then slowly and methodically crush the guinea pig or rabbit it has been given can possibly imagine what a hideous and terrible sight it is. 'Terrible' is no exaggeration.

Anything inevitable and deliberate has always seemed to me to be terrible. How slowly the snakes approached their destined prey, so as to be able to fascinate them and not frighten them at first sight. With what deliberation they crushed them, and with what deliberation their jaws engulfed the still panting victims. It had the inexorable deliberation of the minute hand of a watch. To a superficial observer the hand appears to be stationary, yet in an hour it has traveled right around the dial and timed the last breath of many a poor mortal!"

My interlocutor seemed to become agitated. It made me a little nervous and I furtively measured the distance that separated me from the door and the bell.

Mr. F. noticed that my attention had wandered, but fortunately misunderstood the reason.

"It's nothing," he said. "We shan't be disturbed. Dr. Marchand has left strict orders that we are not to be disturbed." (I, for my part, much regretted that the doctor had extended his consideration quite so far.)

"It is none of my business to describe the nature of our relations. I must however confess that I was completely under the charm of Circe, who exercised her baleful spells on me.

"I realized quite clearly that the only thing which counted with her was her own pleasure, and not mine. But I was so enamored of her that her pleasure was my only pleasure. I was her prisoner. I was taken captive by the invisible threads with which she bound me without my perceiving it. And, would you believe me, I imagined all the time that I was in her debt and owed her everything; and all the time I tried to cancel this imaginary debt by showering on her those trifling gifts which are said to promote mutual affection.

"So as to make quite sure that my gifts would be welcome, I left Miss Hoyet to choose them. This she did; with so much skill, however, that I could almost imagine it was I who had chosen them. In a word, it was a case of the famous tango all over again. I thought I was guiding my partner, and what really happened was that she was making me follow her wherever she wanted to go.

"The first object that attracted her was a tiny ruby displayed in the windows of Cristobald Brothers' strange curiosity shop, where you may purchase butterflies mounted between two sheets of glass, or Portuguese crucifixes, or vast aquamarines or beryls of the color of crystallized angelica.

" 'If that ruby belonged to me, I should have it mounted quite differently,' hinted Alice.

"I bought the stone and offered it to her.

" 'This ruby is of little value because it isn't transparent; that's why I let you offer it to me. But it gives me far more pleasure than a perfectly clear stone. It has exactly the look of a drop of clotted blood.'

"And indeed, when Alice placed the cabochon, which was the size of a pea, on the back of her pale hand, you might have thought that she had been scratched by a bramble and that a large drop of blood had issued from an invisible wound.

"On another occasion it was a rock crystal in which a red tourmaline had been miraculously embedded.

" 'Oh, my dear,' she cried, 'look at this crystal. It's bleeding! Have you ever seen anything so extraordinary? Do you think it will be very expensive? It would be dreadful to think of its falling into the hands of someone who is unable to appreciate the drama going on in that stone.'

"Need I tell you I made my companion the offer of the stone that dripped blood?

"That was how our romance began. Mrs. Hoyet took hardly any interest in it; I had lost much of her goodwill since I had taken up with her daughter.

"One day, however, I found her alone in the hall of my hotel and suggested that we should go and take tea at a pastry cook's.

" 'If you like,' she replied rather coldly.

"When we got there, Mrs. Hoyet declined the offer of tea,

preferring to make it port wine. Under the influence of this tonic she became, I will not say more amiable, but at any rate more ready to talk.

"We spoke, in turn, of New York and Los Angeles, of life in Washington and in Boston, which I said was my favorite town.

"This declaration, which I made in all sincerity, appeared to soften her.

" 'I was born in Boston,' she said.

"When, a few moments later, I took leave of her, after having seen her back to the door of her little house, she looked me straight in the eyes and pronounced this rather enigmatic phrase, the serious import of which was only to become clear to me much later:

" 'My dear boy, don't give way to all of Alice's fancies; don't yield to all her whims.'

"It seemed to me that she purposely underlined the word *all,* as though I should feel and understand the menace implicit in it."

"It was about a month later that Alice and I returned to Cristobald Brothers' curiosity shop and, to pass the time, went over it from top to bottom.

"In a showcase which was less well lit than some of the others and had escaped our attention on other visits, probably because it was in the dark, we found a group of grinning masks from China and Japan, and a few idols of Polynesian origin. They were surrounding a very strange object which I must describe to you. Do you know what a tsantsa is?"

I replied that I did.

"Then that will save my describing it at length," answered Mr. F. "Anyway, I can tell you that this tsantsa was set out in a rather odd fashion.

"On an alabaster base stood a glass stem that disappeared

into the neck of the tiny human head which was no larger than an orange.

"The place where the neck had been severed was concealed by a trimming of hummingbird feathers, the presence of which, so far from attenuating the savage aspect of the trophy, only served to emphasize it. The long hairs, reaching down to the alabaster base, caressed it with the tops of their locks when there was the slightest draft, and thus gave animation to the uncanny little figure. The glass stem only just rested, no doubt, under the arch of the cranium, in the very center of the scalp, so that the head, too, rocked gently up and down whenever there was any displacement of air in the room. I can assure you that this semblance of acquiescence in an inanimate head was, to say the least of it, impressive. Alice Hoyet gazed at the moving object, fascinated by it, and, without knowing she did so, nodded her head just as the tsantsa did. It really seemed to me that she was putting a series of questions to the mummy and receiving satisfactory answers.

" 'There!' said Alice suddenly. 'There is the first thing I've seen for ages that I am really longing to possess. . . . If only—'

"I could not help notice that my lovely friend did not, for once, in a way, resort to her usual technique, which enabled her to make her wishes known by roundabout ways. No, she spoke quite frankly. I also noted that it was not very kind of her to give me to understand how little she valued all the small presents I had been able to make her, up to that moment, in comparison with this new treasure. But what shocked me still more was to discover a young, beautiful and charming girl who could wish to possess so utterly repulsive an object. I did not hide my feelings from her. My observations were not well received.

" 'I don't want *this* relic,' answered Alice, while she turned on me those pale eyes of periwinkle blue the like of which I have never found again, save in the features of very small children. 'No, I don't want *this* relic; the one I want will be rather different. I'll talk to you about it one day when you are a little more amiable.'

"And we left the shop in silence—a silence which I found disturbing, as though it were charged with menace.

"From that day onward Alice was no longer quite the same, at least not with me.

"She was always as friendly—no, I ought to call it tempting—as ever; I never found her more desirable, and I never desired her more than I did then. But there was no more question of my obtaining favors, big or small, which up till then she had dispensed, I must admit, very parsimoniously.

"It is true that we often used to go out and dine together, but all our meetings became—how shall I put it?—dreadfully platonic. So platonic that my nerves suffered badly in consequence, for it is much easier to endure the absence of favors than to lose them when you have once been accustomed to them."

(Now we have it, thought I; this is what has caused the trouble: it's a cause of "suppression of the libido" with its inevitable consequences. How Freud would have loved to hear this story!)

"There was no more flirting between us, no more kissing. Yet Alice would often gaze at me with her clear eyes, and her mouth would smile as much as to say 'When do you want me?'

"I decided to have a word with her about our 'situation.'

"'You are ill, my friend,' she replied. 'It's you who have changed, not I. I'm just the same as ever.'

"But even while she was saying this, she placed her hand on my breast, and gently but firmly prevented my approaching any closer to her. The gesture belied the reassuring words. I was simple enough to open my heart to her mother.

"'I must have done something to displease Alice without knowing what it is. She does not ostensibly avoid me, but I feel as if a glass partition had been set up between us—tangible, though quite invisible.'

"Mrs. Hoyet eyed me with an expression which betrayed no

surprise, though her look seemed tinged with a touch of sadness.

" 'Perhaps this state of affairs is best for you,' she said finally. 'Alice is capricious.'

"And she left me.

"All of a sudden it seemed to me that my behavior had been monstrous. I had never—no, never—discussed plans for the future with my beautiful friend. I had been living in unpardonable egoism in the present, as though it were going to last forever. I had admitted unconsciously that she loved me as much as I loved her, and it had never occurred to me to find what I might call a more conventional solution of the difficulties our free-and-easy relations had given rise to.

"I was on the wrong road, and it was high time to leave it and to make the amends that honor demanded.

"The first time I found myself with Alice, I told her that I realized how wrong I had been, that I felt I owed her my apologies, and I asked her if she would consent to become my wife.

" 'You are ill,' she replied for the second time. 'Aren't you happy to be free, to have no tie binding you to me or any other woman? I for my part want no tie in my life. No possession is as precious as liberty.'

"So, then, I was mistaken. Alice bore me no grudge on account of the nature of our relations, which, nevertheless, might compromise her.

"Rightly or wrongly, I reported our conversation to Mrs. Hoyet, doubtless because in the back of my mind I wanted to whitewash myself a little in her eyes so that I should not look like an unscrupulous seducer.

" 'I should have been happy to welcome you as a son-in-law,' she replied with the calm that never deserted her, 'though . . . you have rather neglected me.'

"Then dropping this light tone, she added:

" 'You are wasting your time. My daughter does not like men. No,' she said, raising her hand as though to banish the shadow of an ugly suspicion. 'No, I don't mean that at all. My daughter does not like *any*one. She only likes *things*.'

"Here again Mrs. Hoyet accentuated *things,* which she pronounced in the emphatic tone that public speakers reserve for the words *Honor, Liberty* and *Duty*.

"The truth then was that Alice liked no one. She only liked things. This meant that her own mother could not flatter herself that she counted for anything in her eyes. Still less had I any sort of existence for her. Or, at least, I only began to exist when her singular mind was filled with an overwhelming longing to possess something, whether it was a blood-red ruby, or a pink tourmaline embedded in a piece of rock crystal.

"That night I slept badly. I even fancy I may not have slept at all. All my life I had dreamed of finding a woman to dominate me, a woman who would love me because I obeyed her. And what I had found was a woman who put up with me because I was of use to her. How humiliating that was!

"I had believed myself to be loved by a woman, and in reality it was I who was in love with a siren. And she made use of me to get what she wanted."

José broke off. He took a handkerchief and mopped his forehead. The evocation of his past life had quite obviously affected him and cost him an effort.

This I wanted to spare him.

"You are tiring yourself," I said to him, "and it's my fault. Wouldn't you rather I came back tomorrow? We'll take up your story at the exact place where you have left it."

"Impossible," replied my host. "How many a time I have run over in my mind the series of misfortunes which have brought me here. If I interrupted the story I am telling you at the point we have reached, I should have to continue the gloomy, implacable sequel on my own, all alone, in this prison chamber, as I have done a thousand times and more. And if you came back tomorrow I should have to take up the thread of the narrative from the beginning, so as to be able to give you the exact sequence of events. No, I beg of you to hear me to the end."

His excitement rather frightened me, but from the convincing way he argued I saw that by staying I should do him less harm than by going.

"I am quite willing to listen to you," I replied.

José F. seemed reassured and went on more calmly.

"The following day a consoling, or rather a comforting, thought gained possession of me. I was free, I was young, I was rich. I could well afford the luxury of having an elusive friend. I could gratify her wishes and win her smiles. In a word, I could give her whatever she liked to ask and receive in exchange for the favors I so highly valued.

"I shall get the better of her, thought I. In reality I was a beaten man, a beaten man who had unconditionally surrendered.

"Alice must have understood the completeness of my surrender, for she approached me straightaway. It looked as though she were trying, by a cheerfulness that did not seem assumed, to make me forget the shadows which had separated us. In point of fact, she was only trying to regain her influence. Her 'caprices,' as her mother called them, were not very alarming. Sometimes a row in a boat by moonlight, or else the purchase of a few rare flowers, more curious than beautiful. I remember perfectly well the day on which a stroll, which had no ostensible object, brought us back again to Cristobald's shop.

"Involuntarily, I thought once more of the famous tango, with myself as her obedient cavalier, in the course of which she had succeeded, without exercising any apparent pressure, in drawing me away as far as possible from the place where her mother awaited her.

"Our walk took us through a labyrinth of little streets without much interest. We wandered about talking of one thing and another, and suddenly came out opposite the flower market in the Rue de Buenos Aires.

"She did not cast a glance at the scented blossoms beautifully arranged in raffia baskets. Making her way round the flower hall, she stopped in front of the window of her favorite shop.

"A phrase rose to my lips so automatically that I was struck by the sound of my own voice after I had uttered it.

" 'Is there anything here that tempts you, my dear Alice?'

"She replied without a moment's hesitation:

" 'You know perfectly well that I want a tsantsa.'

"I had a shock. This beautiful young person, whose sober and harmonious clothes proclaimed her good taste, and whose gait was consistently light and graceful, clung to her morbid inclination and asked—begged, indeed, with a sort of unhealthy insistence—to be given this really frightful object.

"It was too late to turn back. Besides, I no longer had the necessary energy to protest.

" 'Let's go in,' I said to her rather sharply.

" 'But, my good friend,' she calmly replied, 'it isn't *this* tsantsa I want. I want a tsantsa that is the only one of its sort in the world.' Then she remained silent.

" 'I'm afraid I don't quite understand what you mean,' I said. 'All tsantsas are more or less alike, in size and even in expression, and this one seems to be as desirable—forgive me, as little desirable—an example as any other.'

" 'I want a tsantsa unlike any other in the world,' she replied, having made up her mind all at once to overcome her reticence. 'I want a tsantsa prepared from the head of a white man . . . and he must be fair-headed,' she added.

"I could hardly believe my ears.

" 'What a horrible joke! You *are* joking, Alice, aren't you?' said I, feeling a little uncomfortable at the sight of my companion's determined and overcast expression. 'Besides, such a tsantsa doesn't exist,' I added in conclusion, feeling that the joke was in dubious taste and had gone far enough.

" 'Well, then, one has got to be made—that's all,' she replied. And as she walked away from the shop she hummed a Russian song she was fond of and which I had learned from her.

I want what is not in the world;
I want what does not yet exist.

"We went back to Copacabana in silence. I said good-bye to her at her door. Suddenly she kissed me.

"Three days later I found myself by chance—outside Cristobald's shop.

"I entered and made a few trifling purchases of which I had no particular need. I then got into conversation with the good man, who by now knew me well and treated me as a friend, and I discussed the possibility of breeding those sky-blue butterflies with a metallic sheen which are made up into souvenirs of questionable taste for the use of tourists.

" 'Why,' said I, 'do they exterminate these wonderful insects which are becoming more and more rare? You admit it yourself, since you are obliged to raise their price from year to year, when it would be such a simple matter to breed them, as one does silkworms, especially as the food the caterpillars require can be found at the very door of Rio and abounds in the jungle adjoining the "Chinese View." '

" 'No doubt, no doubt,' replied Mr. Cristobald, who agreed with me more, I fear, because he regretted to see one of his sources of revenue shrinking than from any regret at seeing these heavenly butterflies disappear.

"But had I gone there to talk about butterflies? I was aware in a confused kind of way what I had really gone to see him about, and I was secretly ashamed that I was unable either to broach the subject with the astute dealer, or even to admit to myself the reason for my having entered his shop.

"It was only when I had my hand on the latch of the door

that I plucked up the necessary courage to bring out the great question.

" 'What would be the price of a tsantsa like the one you showed us a little while ago?'

" 'It's not for sale,' replied the jeweller, 'or, to speak more plainly, it's no longer for sale.' To soften the disappointment his refusal to sell might cause me, he added: 'The government has forbidden any further dealings in them.'

" 'But where did you purchase it?' I hazarded the shot, hardly expecting a truthful answer. A dealer in curios does not care to divulge the source of his wares. He gave it to me, however.

" 'At Trinidad, in a curiosity shop belonging to a Swiss.'

"And he' let me have his name and address.

"The same evening I wrote to this dealer. As you may imagine, I was neither so simple nor so daring as to mention a trophy owing its existence to the decapitation of a white man. I confined myself to inquiring whether 'in spite of a recent decree' it was still possible by his good offices to procure a tsantsa. I also asked how much 'a curiosity of that sort' would be likely to cost—for a museum, I added, doubtless to exonerate myself in my own eyes, and to give him to understand that, so far as I was concerned, such an object did not interest me. In a postscript, as though it had only just occurred to me since beginning my letter, I added the following question:

" 'Has there ever been, to your knowledge, such a thing as a tsantsa made from the head of a European?' and I awaited his reply.

"To my surprise, I did not have to wait long for it. Three weeks later my correspondence brought me a letter dated from Trinidad."

Mr. F. rose and took from a drawer a letter whose crumpled paper and discolored ink sufficiently denoted its age.

I read it and asked his permission to copy it, to which he was kind enough to agree. The letter from Roche, the man in Trinidad, ran as follows:

Sir,

As you know, any dealing in tsantsas is strictly forbidden, both by the British and the Brazilian governments, with very good reason too. For certain technical details, which I will not describe here, have shown that several tsantsas are of quite recent origin and have probably been prepared, not as more or less legitimate war trophies, but for the sole purpose of satisfying the demands of private collectors.

But as you are inquiring on behalf of a museum, and I possess a good example of a warrior tsantsa, which I can prove was made before the law was promulgated, I can arrange to have it brought for your inspection by a confidential agent who, as luck will have it, has to go to Rio towards the end of this month.

I prefer not to discuss in a letter the price of this exceedingly rare object, but one must obviously take count of the fact that we are dealing with a very "special" kind of curio, the value of which is determined not only by the almost complete secrecy with which it is prepared, but also, and above all, by the difficulty of procuring "the raw material" from which it is fabricated.

Believe me, {etc.}

P.S. The Rev. Father Kirschner, in his work Curiosidad de las Amazonas, *notes the existence of a tsantsa which was made from the head of a white missionary killed by the natives of the banks of the Amazon. Such a thing never has and never will, of course, come into the market.*

Mr. F. had helped me to decipher the letter's faded script.
"I recall," he went on, "I recall how, on receipt of his letter, just as I was reading the last sentence, the refrain of the Russian

song of which Alice was so fond set up insidious echoes in my mind:

> *I want what is not in the world;*
> *I want what does not yet exist.*

And then a feeling of immense peace came over me.

"Alice, I thought, will never have her horrible tsantsa.

"And I was so successful in ridding my mind of the unpleasant problem that I did not even trouble to reply to the letter from Trinidad.

"Ah, sir! Had I replied and brought our dealings to an end, all the evil—Mr. F. dwelled on the word *evil*—would have been avoided. Why did I not write to say that I was not taking this warrior tsantsa?

"A month went by. A happy month. Alice was gentle and tranquil. She granted me just enough of her favors to make me believe that it only depended on me to obtain more.

"Her mother, on the other hand, seemed to avoid me. It was of course my fault, as by my clumsy confidences I had let her perceive that my relations with her daughter were perhaps something more than friendly.

"Once, however, on meeting me in the hall of the hotel, she spoke to me.

" 'Why not travel,' she said to me quite simply. 'Why not travel? It's such a wonderful cure!'

"I recalled a phrase of Jean Cocteau on the subject of the opium smoker:

> Saying to a smoker, "Smoke no more, you'll be
> happier," is the same as saying to Romeo, "Kill
> Juliet, you'll feel much better."

"Travel? Travel by myself? That would be to kill Juliet. No, our shadows were destined to mingle. My life only existed on those terms. We had renewed our daily walks and sometimes pushed them as far as the 'Chinese View,' as the pagoda was called which was built on the granite rock formations surrounding Rio.

"From this charming pavilion one can see the series of bays that frame the town, and one may travel with the eyes and the imagination without having to move.

"It was on returning from one of these excursions that I was addressed by the hall porter at the Copacabana.

" 'A man has been here who wanted to speak to you, sir. He will return this evening.'

" 'What is his name?' I inquired.

" 'He did not leave his name but said you were expecting him,' replied the porter in what was obviously a tone of disapproval. Evidently my visitor was a *persona non grata*.

"I was not expecting anybody that day. Some sort of tout, thought I.

"At nine o'clock in the evening my unknown visitor called again.

"I understood at once why the hotel porter had not approved.

"The visitor, when he appeared, was wearing buffalo leggings which were covered with dust, and for the braided members of the staff of a grand hotel, who are far more intolerant snobs than the guests, that was quite inadmissible.

"Apart from that, his figure was robust and his complexion bronzed. What struck me more was that he was hairless. This absence of hair was not due to the use of the razor, but to the fact that he was naturally beardless, as many Indians are and also some half-castes.

"Without wanting to be questioned, he addressed me in bad Portuguese, interspersed with Spanish and Italian words.

" 'I come from Señor Roche,' said he, pointing to a leather satchel which he carried under his arm.

" 'Roche?' said I, astonished. 'I don't know anyone of that name.'

" '*Si, si*,' he replied, like a man sure of his facts. 'Señor Roche of Trinidad.'

The name of the island wakened memories.

" 'Ah!' said I, 'I understand what you mean or rather of whom you want to talk. Take a seat will you?'

"And, rather intrigued, I pointed to a deserted corner of the bar.

"My visitor opened his satchel and, turning out a silk handkerchief, drew from it with infinite precaution, which reminded me of the delicate gestures a mother would use in handling her newborn baby, an ebony-colored tsantsa.

" 'Pretty! Don't you like it?' cried this strange commercial traveler who seemed enchanted at the horrible perfection of the object he offered me.

"In fact, the warrior head had been reduced by the secret treatment to less than a quarter of its original dimensions. He tried to put it on my knees.

" 'No, no, I don't want it,' I said, pushing away the terrible thing with aversion which was anything but feigned.

"My visitor was not to be put off so easily. He brought out a letter from his pocket. I recognized my own handwriting. It was the letter I had written to Roche a month earlier.

"Mr. Sanchez—that was my visitor's name—marked the postscript with a stroke of his nail, the famous postscript which I had scribbled right at the end of my letter in the hope that by doing so I had minimized its importance.

"Underlined by his sharp and dirty nail, it suddenly acquired capital importance; indeed, it looked as though the whole of the letter had only been written in order to lead up to this postscript.

" 'Do you want a white tsantsa?' he suddenly asked point-blank, bending his face towards mine as though to propose some secret pact.

" 'But,' said I, a little taken aback, 'do you actually happen to have one? I thought that Father Kirschner—'

" 'Father Kirschner?' broke in the man. 'Never heard of him. No, a white tsantsa. As white as'—he was feeling for his words—'as white as ivory!'

"And then I committed the crime.

" 'How much?' I asked.

"I beg your pardon," I interrupted. "I don't understand why you have just used the word *crime*. You bought something which it is forbidden to deal in, I agree. More than that, it was possibly obtained by criminal means. But you were not a guilty party, and if you had not been the purchaser, someone else would have bought it. So you are not guilty!"

It seemed to me that Mr. F. colored slightly. However that may be, I noticed that he made an effort to continue his narrative.

"Sir," he said at last, "the word *crime* is unfortunately the only admissible one. I felt convinced that when Sanchez offered me the white tsantsa and asked a hundred thousand pesos for it, he was not yet in possession of it and that he would have to procure one."

"But, look," I interrupted, "what you are telling me ought to reassure you still more. Seeing that Sanchez had to obtain this anatomical specimen from someone else, that pushes the crime back yet a further stage."

"You do not understand me, because the whole thing is monstrous," replied F. "Sanchez had to obtain his head from tribes on the Amazon; they in turn were not in possession of it, but had to prepare it to order. Do you quite understand me? To order."

The confession was out.

Mr. F. seemed relieved. But with his habitual gesture he mopped his forehead as before, in spite of the cool temperature of the room in which we were sitting.

What could I reply? I kept silent.

After all, I had not come here to argue with a man who, I

had been assured, was a madman, but to listen to his story.

"This visit of Sanchez had taken place in December, and as I heard no more about him during the succeeding months and he gave no sign of life, I came to hope that this individual belonged to the world of nightmares.

"Alice was once more a victim of her intermittent attacks of coldness. *Victim* is perhaps hardly the word, as I am now inclined to think that every attitude she adopted towards me was carefully studied. She seldom gave me the pleasure of her company on my walks, which henceforth I took alone, and she never kissed me anymore; she had never, it is true, bestowed her kisses on me, but she had given me back mine without apparent displeasure.

"When I complained of her coldness, which I did not think I had deserved, she gazed at me with her beautiful childlike eyes without saying a word. Once however she replied with this enigmatic phrase: 'How can I help it? I am disappointed. . . .' And she refused to explain the riddle.

"I gathered that she was alluding to the tsantsa, but as the thought wakened my suspicions of having concluded a disgraceful bargain, as well as horror at having given way to a shameful temptation, I dismissed the explanation as too simple, and for the first time in my life began to practice the famous American slogan: Forget it.

"In spite of taking up this attitude, I began to long for the return of Sanchez, though only a short time before I had so much dreaded it.

"I had a dim suspicion that a great many things depended on his return. Even today I doubt whether Miss Hoyet was really so anxious to have her tsantsa. What attracted her was the idea of making me climb down—capitulate perhaps expresses it better.

"I could not help having a feeling that, if I blindly yielded to her whims, she would no longer hold out against mine. That would be the 'fair exchange,' which is the basis of all sound business. As you see, I am not trying to read poetry into our story, which belonged to the world of the cinema. Above all things, I felt it would put an end to the tension between us which her caprice had created.

"The last hot spells brought on a few cases of yellow fever in the hamlets on the frontiers of Brazil and the neighboring countries to the north. Very sensibly the authorities at once issued further regulations to compel those living in the capital to undergo preventive vaccination.

"I went with Mrs. Hoyet to the immunization pavilion. Alice refused to accompany us.

"That was her undoing, I fancy, for three weeks later she was in the isolation hospital, a victim of the dangerous disease.

"Judge of my agony: I was not allowed to see the patient. At the very moment when she was hanging between life and death, Sanchez arrived on the scene. Once more the hotel porter informed me that a man wished to speak to me, but this time I guessed with whom I had to deal.

"I sent Sanchez a message to come up to my room. He appeared a few minutes later, carrying his inseparable leather satchel, which I eyed on this occasion rather apprehensively. What did it contain?

"But, would you believe it, such is human nature that I took a certain pleasure in his visit. After all, this was the last act of a drama which had been unendurable for me; it was about to be played and I was anxious to see the final fall of the curtain!

"Sanchez, without addressing me with his usual salutations, opened the leather pocket, and with his motherly precautions, which strangely belied the roughness of his appearance, unrolled the few yards of silk in which the tsantsa was wrapped.

"The thing made its appearance. I had a real shock, it was so utterly unlike anything I had expected.

"I do not know why, but I had steeled myself to see the head of a white man with chestnut-colored hair, which would harmonize with the bluish tinge of a close-shaven chin and contrast with the pallor of a sallow complexion.

"But this tsantsa had pale, silky locks of astonishing fineness, which became alive at the slightest movement of the head, as though they belonged to a living body.

"The color of the face was milk-white, and the turned-up nose was dotted with freckles like those one sees on the faces of English youths.

"I immediately got the impression that I was being offered a tsantsa made with the head of a young boy, of a student or, rather, of a growing schoolboy.

"I refused to touch this fragment of corpse (as I called it in my own mind) and begged Sanchez to put it back in the silk from which he had removed it with the gestures of a sentimental conjurer.

"Even through the wrapping I was dimly conscious that this was no antique but something new, horribly new, the freshness of which was due to the actual youthfulness of the sacrificial victim.

"Sanchez's behavior, moreover, reinforced my impression.

" 'I regret,' said he, 'that I cannot accept a hundred thousand cruzeiros. A lot of people had to be made to keep their mouths shut, and that was not as easy as shutting the mouth of the tsantsa. Consciences are very dear. So it will be two hundred thousand cruzeiros that you owe me.'

"I was so disgusted with Sanchez (and with myself) that no sum would have seemed too big at that moment as the price of getting rid of him, and I immediately gave him, without a word of protest, a check for the amount he demanded.

"Sanchez took his departure, leaving the silk wrapping on the table.

"As I was hiding the macabre object in a drawer, the door opened again.

" 'Look,' said Sanchez, who had come back, 'if the National Bank asks what the check is for, say that it is for a magnificent stone.'

"And Sanchez closed the door again.

"Thus the drama ended, and from then onward I should enjoy a more agreeable life. At least I thought so at the time.

"The very next day Mrs. Hoyet, without waiting for the daily visit I paid in order to get news of Alice, who was still kept in quarantine, asked me to come and see her in her house, where, very much to my surprise, I was conducted up to her room.

"The very first words with which she received me, cutting out the usual polite greetings, made me understand the reason for her breaking the rules of correct behavior.

" 'Alice has died,' she said quite simply. 'Will you help me to fulfill all the necessary formalities for the funeral?'

" 'There, there,' she added, seeing me turn pale from the shock. 'Quick! Give yourself a neat whisky; that will set you right again.'

"These were her only words of sympathy."

"I pass in silence over the three following days. The funeral was on a skimpy scale; it was probably fear of contagion that reduced the number of participants to a minimum.

"On the next day but one Mrs. Hoyet told me she had decided to go back to Boston, where a second funeral service would take place. She gave me to understand that her distant relations in Boston would consider my presence at it useless, if not out of place. How could I insist?

"I helped her to obtain a comfortable berth on a ship going to Philadelphia, and I decided to take the first passenger boat available for Europe.

"It seemed to me, in fact, that by putting a long distance between myself and the scenes where so much had happened, I might lighten a little the burden of my past.

"I was deceiving myself. It is precisely here in Marseilles that my general collapse set in. What I am now about to tell you is something very strange indeed. No one is disposed to credit what I say, and all those in whom I have confided have invariably thought that I was out of my mind. I will not ask you to believe me, but only listen to me. One cannot expect anyone to believe in things that are incomprehensible and out of the ordinary."

Mr. F. rose and opened the windows which overlooked the garden. Far away, Notre Dame de la Garde seemed to float in the air. Everything would have spoken of peace and quiet if the solid bars cutting across the landscape had not reminded me of the spot in which we found ourselves. They seemed to warn me, in their own dumb language, to be careful and to avoid taking too literally the stories I had been told.

"It was at Marseilles," F. continued after sitting down again, "that I felt the first onset of the illness which has brought me here.

"Oh, it was nothing serious to begin with; just an occasional migraine which I attributed to a change of diet and of climate. But these headaches became more frequent and more violent. At first they lasted an hour, and I rid myself of them by taking a capsule of aspirin; later on the attacks would continue for several hours and would not yield even to big doses of opiates. I felt as if my head had been taken in a vise and some unseen power were tightening the screw. You may say that was just autosuggestion. Up to a point, I agree, but one day, as I was preparing to go out for my morning stroll and put on my felt hat, I found that it came right down over my ears.

"The barber took too much off last night, thought I. As the hat was an old one, I bought another in the course of my walk, taking care to see that it fitted perfectly.

"Three months later, to my surprise, the new hat in its turn came down over my ears.

"This time I was angry! I had not had my hair cut the day before. I went back to the hatter and vented my ill humor on him. He was very apologetic. 'Since the war,' he explained, 'the felt we get has not the old quality; moreover, the leather used for the linings is too new. If you will allow me to put a cork band inside, that should make it fit all right.' I left the shop reassured.

"Another three months went by. Suddenly I had to accept the evidence. The hat was indeed of a very poor quality and had become much larger in size.

"I gave it to the floor waiter in my hotel, who was obviously delighted to possess a practically new hat, and went to another shop. This time, to avoid trouble, I bought a hat from Lock, the London maker, regardless of the prohibitive value of the pound. You know how carefully these hats are manufactured and at what a price they are sold.

"Well, three months later I had to have the cork lining doubled, and three months later still I put it in the rag bag.

"The truth began to be apparent and to leap to the eye. The top of my head was shrinking.

"The pains, which grew worse and worse, no longer yielded to narcotics. Morphia alone still gave me some relief. And if the drug partially relieved the pain, it was unable to calm my apprehensions. I saw—I beg your pardon, I see—my skull melting, as you might say, beneath my eyes. I was the victim, as I was well aware, of a strange phenomenon which was linked in my imagination, and is still linked today, with the horrible bargain concluded the year before."

I interrupted Mr. F. By so doing I wanted to give him the impression that I was not disputing his way of looking at the matter. That attitude is always wise with madmen, thought I.

"And the head, the tsantsa. What have you done with it?"

"On arrival at Marseilles I presented it to the anthropological museum in the town. The curator expressed himself as very grateful for my gift. You can see it there, if you feel so inclined. As for me, I will never go to look at it again; no, even if I were allowed out from here, I would not go.

"I need not tell you, I suppose," he continued with a note of gratitude in his voice—gratitude due, no doubt, to the fact that he realized I was listening—"that I went to one doctor after another to tell them of my case. My story, of course, strikes them as fantastic. One of these doctors, a friend of my half-brother, cabled to him as head of our family to say how worried he was about me, thus unscrupulously violating the code of professional secrecy. There was a family council. You know the proverb, 'The absent are always in the wrong.' I was interned.

"Would you believe it, I was quite in agreement about my internment, for several reasons. First of all, I considered myself guilty, and this prison that you see appeared to be almost too lenient a treatment for what I always call my 'crime.'

"Besides, I was in cruel pain and am now. Only a nursing home would provide me with the doses of morphia which still procure me a little sleep, and in normal life I could never have obtained it in sufficiently large quantities.

"And then there was another thing. The modification in the shape of my cranium, which, for a long time, only I could see, was becoming apparent to the eyes of the most casual observer. I can tell quite easily. People turn round to stare at me as I pass. My Aztec-like skull puzzles them; it is not only conical but comical."

I made a slight gesture of protest, just out of politeness, I admit.

"For pity's sake, let us quit the subject. You can see for yourself that I have become a figure for Carnival. May Ash Wednesday not be long in coming."

Mr. F. had risen. I understood that the audience was at an end and that he had no more to say to me. Moreover, he seemed exhausted, and I rose in my turn.

"I can assure you that I have been keenly interested in your case. In my eyes you are immensely less guilty than you imagine. Just as Adam would never have plucked the fruit of the tree of knowledge had it not been for the treachery of Eve, you would never have bought the tsantsa but for the tricks and wiles of Miss Hoyet."

"She is dead, sir," put in Mr. F. "Let her rest in peace."

At that moment I realized with some dismay that he was still in love with the woman who had killed him.

The eyes of my interlocutor, sunk in the base of his pyramidal skull, had a strange glint in them. It was with a feeling of having escaped that I took leave of him and shut the door of his room behind me.

"A strange story, in truth, my dear Doctor," said I a few minutes later to Dr. Marchand, who had waited for me in his office. "A kind of persecution mania, associated with an inferiority complex, with the additional complication of masochism. . . ."

"You have clear insight," ventured the doctor.

"Anyhow, the story of the hats is very odd. There we leave the realm of the subjective, don't we?" I asked. "Unless, of course, it's a complete invention."

"No, no," answered the alienist. "I'll tell you what has happened:

"You know that in the newborn child the two halves of the cranium are not joined to one another. It is only some months later that, very gradually, the two edges link up, join and become consolidated.

"In the case of my patient, this joining, for reasons of which I am unaware but which I attribute to a deficiency of calcium, had never taken place. It was only when he was of mature age that the mineral equilibrium was re-established and allowed the normal process to function.

"It is possible that the fact of his having quitted the tropics, which render one liable to anemia, may have hastened the procedure.

"But a suture occurring so late could hardly do otherwise than provoke those pains in the head of which Mr. F. complained and which are perfectly explicable and not in the least imaginary. On the other hand, what was imaginary was the explanation of my patient, who attributed the shrinking of his cranium to his having purchased a tsantsa which he took to have been manufactured (that is the right term to employ) specially for him. From that to an obsession is but a step. And Mr. F. has taken it.

"I was successful in arresting the disease temporarily by inserting some platinum arches between the edges of the bones. The operation was a success because for a year Mr. F. had no more pain. When the pains began to return, I had his head shaved, and beneath where the thick hair had been I could observe that the platinum plates had been bent by the irresistible force of the bone walls coming together.

"Of course, I offered to put in some fresh arches, which would have guaranteed him another year without suffering; at least, that seemed probable. He refused, and absolutely refuses now, and it is not part of my method to use violence towards my patients, especially when they are still capable of reasoning on certain points that concern them, as this man can."

I thanked the doctor and left him. When crossing the threshold of the Villa de la Garde, I had the same feeling of relief that I had experienced a short time before when leaving the room of the sick man.

A few months later I returned to Marseilles. The leisure of a holiday, and curiosity combined, led my steps one day to the anthropological museum of this town.

There I looked in vain in the collection (which was, nevertheless, very well classified) for the white tsantsa presented by "Don José." The tsantsa, I thought, perhaps existed only in the excited imagination of my friend of a day.

The point was worth elucidating, and I sent in my card to the curator of the museum, who received me almost at once.

"Yes, sir," he replied to my question. "Yes, this very curious object was presented to our museum a few years ago by a stranger, who was ill and was a resident in this town. Incidentally, he has died since."

"Died?" I exclaimed.

He nodded and went on:

"It was a unique piece, at any rate when it was handed over to us, but the damp climate of Marseilles was not good for it. The skin of this anatomical specimen, which was probably badly tanned, began to revert after a few months to its original dimensions. After two years it was a life-size, or very nearly life-size, human head that we had in a showcase. More than that, it was evidently the head of a rather charming young boy. It was impossible to look at it without a mixture of pity and horror. Visitors wrote to protest, with good reason.

"The following detail will show you how different the head had at that time become from the tiny doll-like head we had accepted as a curiosity. We decided that its proper place was no longer in our museum, but in a graveyard. We gave it into the care of a priest, who took it on himself to have it buried, though I am unaware of the exact spot."

I took my leave and decided to recall myself to the memory of Dr. Marchand.

I described to him the strange impression produced on me by the discovery of the change brought about in the white tsantsa, which grew bigger in proportion as the skull of the late Mr. F. diminished.

"I don't quite see what you are getting at," replied the doctor, who seemed rather put out by my visit.

"You surely don't mean to imply that my patient was right in establishing a connection between his own deformity, or rather his progressive deformation, and that of a museum specimen the recollection of which haunted his unhinged mind?"

What was I to answer?

In the eyes of science and men of science, the doctor was right. And yet . . .

"MAN OVERBOARD!"

WINSTON CHURCHILL

IT WAS A LITTLE AFTER half-past nine when the man fell overboard. The mail steamer was hurrying through the Red Sea in the hope of making up the time which the currents of the Indian Ocean had stolen. The night was clear, though the moon was hidden behind clouds. The warm air was laden with moisture. The still surface of the waters was only broken by the movement of the great ship, from whose quarter the long, slanting undulations struck out, like the feathers from an arrow shaft, and in whose wake the froth and air bubbles churned up by the propeller trailed in a narrowing line to the darkness of the horizon.

There was a concert on board. All the passengers were glad to break the monotony of the voyage, and gathered around the piano in the companion-house. The decks were deserted. The man had been listening to the music and joining in the songs. But the room was hot, and he came out to smoke a cigarette and enjoy a breath of the wind which the speedy passage of the liner created. It was the only wind in the Red Sea that night.

The accommodation ladder had not been unshipped since leaving Aden, and the man walked out onto the platform, as onto a balcony. He leaned his back against the rail and blew a puff of smoke into the air reflectively. The piano struck up a lively turn, and a voice began to sing the first verse of "The Rowdy Dowdy Boys." The measured pulsations of the screw were a subdued but additional accompaniment. The man knew the song. It had been the rage at all the music halls, when he had started for India seven years before. It reminded him of the brilliant and busy streets he had not seen for so long, but was soon to see again. He was just going to join in the chorus, when the railing, which had been insecurely fastened, gave way suddenly with a snap, and he fell backwards into the warm water of the sea amid a great splash.

For a moment he was physically too much astonished to think. Then he realized that he must shout. He began to do this even before he rose to the surface. He achieved a hoarse, inarticulate, half-choked scream. A startled brain suggested the word "Help!" and he bawled this out lustily and with frantic effort six or seven times without stopping. Then he listened.

> *Hi! hi! clear the way*
> *For the Rowdy Dowdy Boys.*

The chorus floated back to him across the smooth water, for the ship had already passed completely by. And as he heard the music a long stab of terror drove through his heart. The possibility that he would not be picked up dawned for the first time on his consciousness. The chorus started again:

> *Then—I—say—boys,*
> *Who's for a jolly spree?*
> *Rum—tum—tiddley—um,*
> *Who'll have a drink with me?*

"Help! help! help!" shrieked the man, in desperate fear.

"MAN OVERBOARD!"

Fond of a glass now and then,
Fond of a row or noise;
Hi! hi! clear the way
For the Rowdy Dowdy Boys!

The last words drawled out faint and fainter. The vessel was steaming fast. The beginning of the second verse was confused and broken by the ever-growing distance. The dark outline of the great hull was getting blurred. The stern light dwindled.

Then he set out to swim after it with furious energy, pausing every dozen strokes to shout long wild shouts. The disturbed waters of the sea began to settle again to their rest. The widening undulations became ripples. The aerated confusion of the screw fizzed itself upwards and out. The noise of motion and the sounds of life and music died away.

The liner now was but a single fading light on the blackness of the waters and a dark shadow against the paler sky.

At length, full realization came to the man, and he stopped swimming. He was alone—abandoned. With the understanding, his brain reeled. He began again to swim, only now instead of shouting he prayed—mad, incoherent prayers, the words stumbling into one another.

Suddenly a distant light seemed to flicker and brighten. A surge of joy and hope rushed through his mind. They were going to stop—to turn the ship and come back. And with the hope came gratitude. His prayer was answered. Broken words of thanksgiving rose to his lips. He stopped and stared after the light—his soul in his eyes. As he watched it, it grew gradually but steadily smaller. Then the man knew that his fate was certain. Despair succeeded hope. Gratitude gave place to curses. Beating the water with his arms, he raved impotently. Foul oaths burst from him, as broken as his prayers—and as unheeded.

The fit of passion passed, hurried by increasing fatigue. He became silent—silent as was the sea, for even the ripples were subsiding into the glassy smoothness of the surface. He swam on mechanically along the track of the ship, sobbing quietly to himself, in the misery of fear. And the stern light became a tiny speck, yellower but scarcely bigger than some of the stars, which here and there shone between the clouds.

Nearly twenty minutes passed, and the man's fatigue began to change to exhaustion. The overpowering sense of the inevitable pressed upon him. With the weariness came a strange comfort. He need not swim all the long way to Suez. There was another course. He would die. He would resign his existence since he was thus abandoned. He threw up his hands impulsively and sank. Down, down he went through the warm water. The physical death took hold of him and he began to drown. The pain of that savage grip recalled his anger. He fought with it furiously. Striking out with arms and legs he sought to get back to the air. It was a hard struggle, but he escaped victorious and gasping to the surface. Despair awaited him. Feebly splashing with his hands, he moaned in bitter misery—

"I can't—I must. O God! Let me die."

The moon, then in her third quarter, pushed out from behind the concealing clouds and shed a pale, soft glitter upon the sea. Upright in the water, fifty yards away, was a black triangular object. It was a fin. It approached him slowly.

His last appeal had been heard.

SO YOU WON'T TALK

ıllıı

MANUEL KOMROFF

ON THE SAME DAY that Handsome Dan shot the sergeant of detectives, the newspapers announced that some Russian scientists had made a wonderful discovery. It was a small news item hidden away, and related to an experiment on a dog which employed great skill in surgery.

The object of the experiment was to show that the brain of the animal could be kept alive by an artificial heart constructed mechanically.

At any rate, whatever the details were, it was all hailed as an important discovery in the scientific world; but what was a discovery in the scientific world compared to Handsome Dan with his criminal record a mile long! When he shot the sergeant of detectives, he went right on the front page of every paper in the country.

All this everyone already knows, and everyone also knows how Dan was trapped in the apartment of one of his lady friends. These details need not be repeated here. Handsome Dan was put through the works. But, faithful to the code of his lawless world, he would not speak.

Captain Quill walked up and down in front of the prisoner. The questioning had been long and strenuous. Finally he drew his chair up close to the criminal and said in quite a confidential tone: "I tell you, Danny, one thing is certain. You can't kill an officer of the law and get away with it. And one thing more is certain. The sergeant and I were very close friends. We had been to war together and we were in the trenches together. And so, Danny, handsome as you are, you've got to come clean. We've got to know who was with you. Will you talk, or won't you talk? *Who* was with you?"

"I don't know."

"If you know what is good for you, you will talk."

"I don't know."

"Who?"

"I don't know!"

Captain Quill had saved the newspapers describing the shooting of the sergeant, and it was in these papers that he noticed the account of the important scientific discovery. He spoke to the ambulance doctor about it, and the ambulance doctor did not seem to know very much; however, he knew a man who was connected with the university who could give the captain a good deal of information. The information that Captain Quill received, however, he did not disclose.

Three months later, a little Russian doctor arrived in town. He had a Vandyke beard, gold-rimmed spectacles, and he was dressed in a very funny collar and necktie. He wore those old-fashioned detachable cuffs that were always loose and falling down over his hands. He had evidently been brought over for something very special, and his mission was kept a great secret. At the hotel the register was signed for him as Dr. Smith from Moscow. Of course this was an assumed name, for no doubt his own name was hard to pronounce and impossible to spell. And so they let it go at that and called him Dr. Smith.

However, during the first few days the Russian doctor was not at all satisfied with the object of his mission, for the hotel clerk said that he was constantly packing his bag ready to leave, and that Captain Quill was trying his best to persuade him against it. One day they drove out in an automobile to the university and saw Professor Fenmore of the Medical School, and then they came back, and he seemed reconciled. At least the clerk of the hotel heard him say to Captain Quill in very good English: "You must understand, Captain, I am a scientific man and for science—I'll do everything. But if it is not for a scientific purpose, then—nothing. You understand. That is my life. That is what I live for."

Captain Quill nodded and said: "Certainly, I understand. You are quite right, Doctor, and you will go ahead and demonstrate your experiment to the university."

The little Russian replied: "Yes. But it will be for demonstration only."

Now the doctor set to work. Two assistants from the hospital went all over town buying all kinds of things: everything from four or five small motors, the kind that are used to run sewing machines, to small cogwheels and fine rubber tubing. The doctor worked in the corner of one of the laboratories of the city hospital.

His main assistant, oddly enough, was not a laboratory worker at all, but a Swedish handyman who was a combination orderly, machinist, carpenter and plumber. He had been some years in the city hospital, and whatever he did, especially his metalwork, was beautifully executed and nicely finished.

Several days before the date set for the execution of Handsome Dan, Captain Quill went into the death house and stood before the prisoner's cell.

"Danny," he said, "you can save yourself a lot of trouble, and this is the last chance I give you. You know very well that I'm not going to rest until I find that other fellow, and so you'd better talk now; for in a couple of days they're going to finish you off and I can tell you now, Danny, you're going to have the swellest finish that ever a man had. And maybe you're not going to like it so much. And so if you want an easy exit, take my advice and talk now."

Handsome Dan smiled. He knew very well that his end was close at hand. He said: "They can't do worse than kill me."

"I tell you, Danny, you're going to talk and that's all there is about it."

"OK, Captain. You know."

"Yes," he said angrily, "I know." And with that he marched out of the death house.

The execution of Handsome Dan took place at six o'clock in the morning. Only a few newspapermen had been invited for this party and the account, simple and brief, was printed in all newspapers. The affair seemed kind of hurried, and the prison doctor had his stethoscope ready and pronounced him dead in very short order. The rope was quickly cut and his body removed at once to the hospital.

In the hospital nothing could be seen. Everything was going on behind closed doors, and these doors were locked with locks almost as large as a bank safe. The Swedish handyman and the Russian doctor were working behind these closed doors, and with them was the corpse of Handsome Dan. They worked all that afternoon and far into the night, and at six o'clock in the morning, exactly twenty-four hours after the trap had been sprung underneath the scaffold, the Russian doctor called Captain Quill on the telephone and said everything was ready.

Quill got into his clothes and drove over to the university to get hold of Professor Fenmore, for that had been his arrangement with the Russian doctor. The work was being done for the scientific world as a demonstration, and therefore the professor from the university was to be the first. All this seemed quite unnecessary to Captain Quill, but a bargain was a bargain.

They came to the locked door of the room. The Swedish handyman answered their knock and he spoke through the door: "The doctor wants to know who is with you."

"The professor is with me and no one else."

Then the bolts were drawn and the two men entered the room. There it was all before them, and the doors were quickly locked.

The Russian doctor spoke to the professor. "It's a good specimen."

On top of a cabinet, especially built for the purpose and containing machinery necessary to pump the blood and keep it at its right temperature and pressure, containing glass tubes, graduates, rubber piping, two electric motors and the maze of intricate apparatus—on top of this cabinet, surrounded by a short glass collar, embedded in two inches of paraffin, was the dismembered head of Handsome Dan. But it showed no signs of life.

Was it alive, or was it dead?

The Russian doctor washed his hands in the sink. He lathered them hard with soap and he scrubbed with a big nailbrush and he dipped his hands in the basin containing some antiseptic solution and dried them on a clean towel.

He put on his coat and he rubbed his hands together and smiled and said to the university professor: "There it is." And he spoke to him in scientific language, and he used such words as "the sternomastoid muscle, and the trapezius is left extra long because it shrinks quickly, and the external jugular is connected directly with the electric heart. I removed the lymphatic glands at once to prevent their swelling and the pulse remains here, as you can notice."

He placed a finger on the jawbone of the head, just one inch in front of the angle of the jaw, and he took out his watch and counted for fifteen seconds. It was beating as it should beat, and the professor also put his finger to that special place on the bone of the jaw and felt the pulse while the Russian doctor warned him: "Gently. The wax is not hard yet. In a little while it will respond to stimulus. It will take another few hours. You are the first, Professor, in America to witness this demonstration. And everything I have done here is clearly in detail described in my articles."

The body from which the head had been taken was on a stretcher at one side of the room and was covered over with a black oilcloth. There were a lot of instruments and tools and all kinds of anatomical paraphernalia that the handyman, well accustomed to hospital things, was busy cleaning up.

The two doctors spoke freely to each other, but Quill could hardly say a word. This was something that had never happened before and, scientific or not scientific, it was being done for one purpose, and he was impatient and he could not wait; and yet he recognized that it was a feat most unusual and coughed aloud to attract the attention of the little Russian doctor. And he shook his head and said: "I congratulate you, Doctor."

"In a few hours we will begin to stimulate it and then, I believe, late this afternoon or tonight you may come back."

That is how it was. The Swedish mechanic watched the instruments that regulated the temperature, pressure and the speed of the electric pump. He did not leave that cabinet for more than one minute at a time. But the Russian doctor, after his work had been accomplished, paid very little attention to anything but sat in one corner of the room and made notes in a journal, and he made little drawings of anatomical details, of tied-up blood vessels and nerves, and of the little connections that he employed to join the head to the mechanical heart.

At six o'clock that night Captain Quill arrived.

The head had now taken on a bluish color and the lips were swollen. The face had been washed with a small sponge and seemed very clean. The mouth was a little bit open, the eyes were slightly open, but the head did not breathe. Yet it was alive. The hair looked dull, as though it were a wig.

Quill spoke. "You look very handsome. Can you hear me, Danny?"

The doctor said: "You must stand closer and talk louder."

"Can you hear me, Danny?" shouted Quill.

The lips moved slightly and the head spoke very faintly. "Let me die."

"Can you see what we did for you, Danny? We fixed you up very nice."

The head replied: "Let me die."

"Can you see, Danny?"

"Yes, I can see. For God's sake, let me die."

"Did you see what the rest of you looks like, you skunk?" said Quill, pointing to the headless corpse covered with black oilcloth.

"I don't care. Let me die."

"So you'd like to die, would you, Danny?"

"Yes," spoke the head.

"It cost me four thousand bucks to keep your stinking corpse alive!"

"Let me die, for God's sake!"

"All right, you dastardly scoundrel. Now, who was with you? Who was it, or by God I'll keep you here forever. We got enough blood to keep you alive for weeks. And this is only the beginning. Who was with you?"

"For God's sake, let me die."

A few drops of dark blood, almost black, leaked out of the mouth and fell in the paraffin trough in which the head was imbedded.

For a moment all was silent and the head again whispered: "For God's sake, let me die."

"All right, you fiend. Who was with you?"

The head hesitated. Then it spoke. "It was that punk Guido. Now let me die, for God's sake."

"You're sure? Say it again. Was it that punk Guido? There's no mistake about it?"

"No mistake," echoed the head. "Let me die."

"In one hour, if what you say is true, we'll turn off the pump."

"It's true," said the head.

Fifteen minutes later they picked up Guido in a poolroom. He swore he was innocent, that he never knew Handsome Dan and that they never had gone out together.

But Quill said: "Come along with me."

He took him to the hospital and led him into the room where the head was being kept alive by the electric heart.

"Now, you stand here," said Quill, "and listen."

Then he shouted loud to the head: "All right, Danny, can you see that punk?"

"Yes, that's him," said the head. "For God's sake, let me die."

Guido turned as white as a sheet. He fell to his knees and jabbered his prayers in Italian. He went almost mad and was removed from the room crying hysterically. He was uncontrollable and they had to give him something to keep him from jumping.

When they got him quiet, he confessed. He told everything.

Quill went to the room and said: "All right, Doctor, you can turn off the switch any time you like."

But the doctor was indignant. His wonderful specimen and all his marvelous work had not yet been seen by the scientific men, and he was waiting for them to arrive.

And so, for the glory of science, the head of Handsome Dan was kept alive twenty-four hours longer.

THE MISTAKE

FIELDEN HUGHES

WHEN I WAS the Medical Superintendent at the Applesett Private Mental Hospital, there was one patient who had been there so long that he was, in that respect as well as in one other, something of an institution. He was a silent man and gave so little trouble that he was in a class apart. He was there, so his record showed, at his own request and at his own expense. He was without near relations, and nobody ever visited him or showed the faintest interest in him, except for many doctors, pathologists, and psychologists to whom he was of vast clinical interest.

Before he entered our hospital, he had been an obscure parson in some West Country village, unknown to any but his few parishioners. After he came to us, unaware of it though he was, he achieved a wide fame in medical circles. For the simple fact about him was that *he never slept.* Every night for a considerable time he used to retire and read quite naturally, and five minutes later would rise from his bed as if he had been asleep for hours. After a time he gave up all idea of going to bed, and treated the night the same as the day.

There was no point in trying to impede him in the habit of twenty-four hours of complete wakefulness, and so a room was placed at his disposal, a room—at his urgent request—without a bed. Usually he spent the night reading or writing, and the sheets of paper he covered he allowed no one to see. Occasionally he would escape from the house during the night, after showing noticeable restlessness for a period. These escapes were always at the same time of the year—in mid-October; and always he was found in the same place—the churchyard in Applesett village. This fact we attributed to some connection in his mind with his former profession. But this became clear when he died, which he did prematurely. For the phenomenon of total insomnia, interesting though it was to us as doctors, was inevitably the cause of quicker wear of his bodily tissues, and this though he was one of the biggest, most powerful men I have ever seen. In youth, he must have been a tremendously strong man. I was always thankful that so muscular a fellow was a quiet inmate. I used to wonder how the attendants would have been able to handle him if he had become violent. But he never did, and we were all truly sorry when he died in his fortieth year. Among his effects, brought to my office after the removal of his body, was a large envelope containing many sheets of paper. It was addressed to me, and marked *Not to be opened till after my death*. I opened the packet, took out the scribbled sheets and read what follows:

When I was the Vicar of St. Alpha's Church in the village of Smeritone, I was happy enough. I could have said I was completely happy except for one man in the village. That man was my warden, Admiral Sir Anthony Vilpert. It was one of those strange cases of complete natural antipathy. We hated one another for no reason that either of us could have given. I hated his very appearance. He was a very thin man with white moustache and beard, the latter thin, like himself, and pointed. I privately called him the "White Goat," for he was pale, with light blue eyes. His voice, so unlike the voice of a sea-going man, was a bleat, and how odious its sound became to me. We bickered and differed about every parish matter, and I found that he was in the wicked habit of talking about me to my detriment behind my back, making mischief and doing all he could to poison people's minds against me, especially newcomers, before I had time to correct by visitation the vile impressions he constantly gave them.

My hatred of the White Goat became an obsession. I found myself thinking about him with loathing. His image would come before my mind in the silence of my study, and I had to avert my eyes from him when I was taking services in church. He filled me with fear as well as hatred, for the expression in those pale eyes told me that there was no evil turn he would not do me if he had the opportunity. I fell into mortal sin, for I murdered him in my heart many a time, so that I could hardly read certain passages of Scripture without feeling condemned in the face of the congregation. Then I would imagine that he could read my heart, and that thin face would seem to smile bitterly at me and defy me.

One day a message came to the vicarage that the White Goat was dangerously ill. I could not repress a terrible hope. However, I set out to his house, but, by the mercy of Heaven, he was dead before I could reach his bedside. And I was overjoyed. To my horror, I was happier than I had ever been.

The day of his funeral arrived, and I met the cortège at the lych gate. As I slowly walked before the coffin to the church door, I heard a tapping sound. My blood chilled as the certainty came to my mind that the tapping came from within the coffin. I dismissed the idea and walked on. It could not be. It was my imagination. It was some weird echo of my hatred of the man. As we moved solemnly up the aisle, I heard the faint sound again. *Tap tap.* Then three more. *Tap, tap, tap.* There was no doubt. I waited for the bearers to act. They must have heard those dreadful sounds even as I had done. One of them would cry out. They would put down the coffin. They would open it, there in the church. But nothing happened, except that I heard the sounds once more, like a muffled, distant drum, I felt faint and had to force my legs to bear me up and on. The dreadful truth was clear. He was not dead. And only I had heard his frantic signals to return to the world.

I cannot tell, even here, of the tumult of my feelings. A terrible sense of his being in my power, there in his coffin, seized me, a glorious power. The thought rushed through my mind like a swift flame that I was a murderer who could never be detected. I who had killed him so often in my thoughts was able now to kill him with a sort of horrible innocence. He was the prisoner of my ears, alone and helpless, dependent for his delivery from the most gruesome bondage upon my silent tongue. The injuries he had done me, the calumnies he had spoken of me, the hatred he had shown to me, all hung upon my lips like locks and bars against my speaking. I seemed to see him lying there, his pale eyes wide open with fear, imploring me to mercy and the release of forgiveness. I saw him as if the coffin lid were made of glass. And with hatred in my heart, I refused his dumb appeal, condemning him to the cruellest of all deaths, a living entombment, a joining of him with the dead before his time, an inescapable, inexorable darkness. Then a kind of healing sanity returned to me. If none other there present had heard the tapping, the quiet frenzy of imprisonment, it must be my imagination.

Calmly and coldly, I went on with my duties. I saw him lowered into his grave. The cold damp afternoon lay silent round us—us living, upon whose brows the wisps of autumn mist were like the exhalations of death. The fragments of soil fell on the coffin thudding, as if we were knocking his outer door in response to his inner tapping. Perhaps he heard them, and hailed them with a momentary thin hope, like a miner entombed in the dark caverns of his mine. And then I heard it again, fainter this time, almost lost amongst the sounds of the soil falling on the coffin.

I turned away and left the group of mourners at the graveside. As I sat in my comfortable study by the fire, the afternoon closed in and the shadows of night gathered. I drew the curtains over my windows, and as I did so, I glanced towards the darkening churchyard. My thoughts seemed suspended. I was living, but numb. I had tea, and wrote a number of letters, as if I were not myself but somebody else. I felt as if a spring were tightly coiled inside me. When I retired, about ten o'clock, the vicarage was very silent. My housekeeper was away overnight, and I locked the doors and went upstairs. I read till half past ten and then fell asleep. Suddenly I was awake, as if I had slept for many hours. I looked at my watch. The time was twenty minutes to eleven. I was wholly refreshed and knew I should sleep no more. The spring had uncoiled inside me. I lay awake in the darkness, as if waiting for something or someone. The church clock struck the quarter, and as if an order had been given me, I knew what I had to do. I rose and dressed. What I had to do, I must do alone. I could not seek any earthly aid. I must know the truth, and there was nobody to help me.

I went downstairs, unlocked the back door, and stepped out into the damp air. The night was still and pitch-black. I went to the hut where the sexton kept his tools. I lit his lantern and took his shovel with me to the newly filled-in grave under the trees. I was young and exceptionally strong then, and I had the night before me. The only sound in the black churchyard was the occasional drip of water from the branches of trees. I could hardly see the bulk of the church against the black sky. I stood the lamp on the ground and taking off my coat, I began to reopen the grave where the White Goat lay. If I had been mistaken about the sounds from the coffin, I must know it, for the peace of the rest of my life. If I had been right, then I must do what I could to redress the wrong I had done. I must find him and restore him, even though the two enemies should meet alone in the black night of the churchyard, the one in his premature shroud, the other in his costume of gravedigger.

Chilly though the night, the sweat poured from my body, and I took off shirt and vest. The clock chimed the night along, shocking me each time it made its solemn sound, as if it were watching me at my horrid work. The earth piled up on the sides of the grave, and I slowly sank down into the pit I was digging. At length, my shovel struck the coffin lid. I cleared away the soil as far as I could, and then I made myself a recess where I could brace myself to tear away the lid. The night closed around me and above as if it were itself a tomb. I had not realized the impossibility of raising the coffin alone, nor the great difficulty of pulling away the lid. Somehow, by taking out the screws and using my spade as a lever, I forced the top to one side. I reached up for my lantern and stared at what lay within. There was my enemy, the man I had hated. The faint beams of my lantern fell upon him. The most terrible feeling gripped me. I knew in that moment what death is: dark, silent, mysterious, yes, but appallingly silly. I began to shake with laughter. I could not let it out in peals in his presence. I scrambled out of the grave and began feverishly filling it in with the earth I had piled around. I had never worked so hard or so fast. A kind of deathly rhythm fell upon my strokes . . . *cover it up . . . fill it in . . . hide it away* . . . and all the time I laughed till I ached. What a mistake it all was.

I had seen for myself. The White Goat was dead. *But he was lying on his side.*

GREEN THOUGHTS

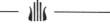

JOHN COLLIER

THE ORCHID had been sent among the effects of his friend, who had come by a lonely and mysterious death on the expedition. Or he had bought it among a miscellaneous lot, "unclassified," at the close of the auction. I forget which, but one or the other it certainly was; moreover, even in its dry, brown, dormant root state, this orchid had a certain sinister quality. It looked, with its bunched and ragged projections, like a huge dead insect, or a rigid yet a gripping hand, hideously gnarled, or a grotesquely whiskered, threatening face. Would you not have known what sort of an orchid it was?

Mr. Mannering did not know. He read nothing but catalogues and books on fertilizers. He unpacked the new acquisition with a solicitude absurd enough in any case, towards any orchid, or primrose either, in the twentieth century, but idiotic, foolhardy, doom-eager, when extended to an orchid thus come by, in appearance thus. And in his traditional obtuseness he at once planted it in what he called "the Observation Ward," facetious fellow! a hot-house built against the south wall of his dumpy red dwelling. Here he set always the most interesting additions to his collection, and especially weak and sickly plants, for there was a glass door in his study wall through which he could see into this hothouse, so that the weak and sickly plants could encounter no crisis without his immediate knowledge and his tender care.

This plant, however, proved hardy enough. At the ends of thick and stringy stalks, it opened out bunches of darkly shining leaves, and soon it spread in every direction, usurping so much space that first one, then another, then all its neighbors had to be removed to a hothouse at the end of the garden. It was, Cousin Jane said, a regular hop-vine. The comparison was little to the point. At the ends of the stalks, just before the leaves began, were set groups of tendrils, which hung idly, serving no apparent purpose. Mr. Mannering thought that very probably these were vestigial organs, a heritage from some period when the plant had been a climber. But when were the vestigial tendrils of an ex-climber half or a quarter so thick and strong?

After a long time, sets of tiny buds appeared here and there among the extravagant foliage. Soon they opened into small flowers, miserable little things; they looked like flies' heads. How disappointed I should have been, and you would too, I hope, or Doyle and Wells have lived and writ in vain. One naturally expects a large, garish, sinister bloom, like a sea anemone, or a Chinese lantern, or a hippopotamus yawning, on any important orchid. Should it be an unclassified one as well, I think one has every right to insist on a sickly and overpowering scent into the bargain.

Mr. Mannering did not mind at all. Indeed, apart from his joy in being the discoverer and godfather of a new sort of orchid, he felt only a mild and scientific interest in the fact that the paltry blossoms were so very much like flies' heads. Could it be to attract other flies for food or as fertilizers? But then, why like their heads?

It was a few days later that Cousin Jane's cat disappeared. This was a great blow to Cousin Jane, but Mr. Mannering was not, in his heart of hearts, greatly sorry. He had not been fond of the cat, for he could not open the smallest chink in a glass roof, for ventilation, but that creature would squeeze through somehow to enjoy the warmth, and in this way it had broken many a tender shoot. But before poor Cousin Jane had lamented two days, something happened that so engrossed Mr. Mannering that he had no mind left at all with which to sympathize with her afflictions, nor to make at breakfast kind and hypocritical enquiries after the lost cat. A strange new bud appeared on the orchid. It was clearly evident that there would be two quite different sorts of bloom on this one plant, as sometimes happens in such fantastic corners of the vegetable world, and that the new flower would be very different in size and structure from the earlier ones. It grew bigger and bigger, till it was as big as one's fist.

And just then, it could never have been more inopportune, an affair of the most unpleasant, the most distressing nature summoned Mr. Mannering to town. It was his wretched nephew, in trouble again, and this time so deeply and so very disgracefully that it took all Mr. Mannering's generosity, and all his influence too, to extricate the worthless young man. Indeed, as soon as he saw the state of affairs, he told the prodigal that this was the very last time he might expect assistance, that his vices and his ingratitude had long cancelled all affection between them, and that for this last helping hand he was indebted only to his mother's memory, and to no faith on the part of his uncle either in his repentance or his reformation. He wrote, moreover, to Cousin Jane, to relieve his feelings, telling her of the whole business, and adding that the only thing to do was to cut the young man off entirely. He begged her, also, to send immediate news of any development on the part of his orchid.

When he got back to Torquay, Cousin Jane had disappeared. The situation was extremely annoying. Their only servant was a cook, who was very old, and very stupid, and very deaf. She suffered, besides, from an obsession, due to the fact that for many years Mr. Mannering had had no conversation with her in which he had not included an impressive reminder that she must always, no matter what might happen, keep the big kitchen stove up to a certain pitch of activity. For this stove, besides supplying the house with hot water, heated the pipes in the Observation Ward, to which the daily gardener who had charge of the other hothouses had no access. By this time she had come to regard her duties as stoker as her chief raison d'être, and it was difficult to penetrate her deafness with any question which her stupidity and her obsession did not somehow transmute into an enquiry after the stove, and this, of course, was especially the case when Mr. Mannering spoke to her. All he could disentangle was what she had volunteered on first seeing him, that his cousin had not been seen for three days, that she had left without saying a word. Mr. Mannering was perplexed and annoyed, but, being a man of method, secretary, indeed, of his county's Lodge of the Royal Antediluvian Order of Orchid Growers, he thought it best to postpone further enquiries until he had refreshed himself a little after his long and tiring journey. A full supply of energy was necessary to extract any information from the old cook; besides, there was probably a note somewhere. It was only natural that before he went to his room, Mr. Mannering should peep into the hothouse, just to make sure that the wonderful orchid had come to no harm during the inconsiderate absence of Cousin Jane. As soon as he opened the door, his eyes fell upon the bud; it had changed in shape very considerably, and had increased in size to the bigness of a human head. It is no exaggeration to state that Mr. Mannering remained rooted to the spot, with his eyes fixed upon this wonderful bud, for fully five minutes.

But, you will ask, why did he not see her clothes on the floor? Well, as a matter of fact, to be perfectly plain and straightforward (it is a delicate point), there were no clothes on the floor. To avoid all shilly-shallying, I must tell you that Cousin Jane, though of course she was thoroughly, entirely estimable in every respect, though she was well over forty, too, was given to the study, and in fact to the practice, of certain of the very latest ideas on the dual culture of the soul and body. Swedish, and German, neo-Greek and all that. You will understand, no doubt. And the orchid house was the warmest place available. I must proceed with the order of events.

Mr. Mannering at length withdrew his eyes from this stupendous bud, and (disciplined in his pleasures as all great souls are) decided that he must temporarily abandon this . . . this positive Peak in Darien, and devote his attention to the grey exigencies of everyday life. But although his body dutifully ascended the stairs, heart, mind and soul all remained, like the three kings of old, in adoration of the plant. Here we see another side to Mr. Mannering's character. Although he was philosophical to the point of insensibility over the miserable smallness of the earlier flowers, yet he was now as much gratified by the magnitude of the great new bud as you or I might be. Is not the orchid grower a man with a heart—like you? Hence, it was not unnatural that Mr. Mannering, while in his bath, should be full of the most exalted visions of the blossoming of his heart's darling, his vegetable godchild. It would be the largest known, by far: complex as a dream, or dazzlingly simple. It would open like a dancer, or like the sun rising. Why, it might be opening at this very moment! At this thought Mr. Mannering could restrain himself no longer; he rose from the steamy water, and, wrapping his bath-towel robe about him, hurried down to the hothouse, scarcely staying to dry himself, though he was subject to colds.

The bud had not yet opened; it still reared its unbroken head among the glossy, fleshy foliage, and he now saw what he had had no eyes for previously, how very exuberant that foliage had grown. Suddenly he realized with astonishment that this huge bud was not that which had appeared before he went away. That one had been lower down on the plant. Where was it now, then? Why, this new thrust and spread of foliage concealed it from him. He walked across and discovered it. It had opened into a bloom. And as he looked at this bloom, his astonishment grew to stupefaction, one might say to petrification, for it is a fact that Mr. Mannering remained rooted to the spot, with his eyes fixed on the flower, for fully fifteen minutes. The flower was an exact replica of the head of Cousin Jane's lost cat. The similitude was so exact, so lifelike, that Mr. Mannering's first movements, after the fifteen minutes, was to seize his bath-towel robe, to draw it about him, for he was a modest man, and the cat, though bought for a tom, had proved to be quite the reverse. I relate this to show how much character, spirit, *presence,* call it what you will, there was upon this floral cat's face. But although he made to seize his bath-towel robe, it was too late. He could not move; the new lusty foliage had closed in unperceived, the too lightly dismissed tendrils were everywhere upon him. He gave a few weak cries and sank to the ground, and there, as the Mr. Mannering of ordinary life, he passes out of this story. Just fancy!

Mr. Mannering sank into a coma, into an insensibility so deep that a black eternity passed before the first faint elements of his consciousness reassembled themselves in his brain. For of his brain the centre of a new bud was being made. Indeed, it was two or three days before this at first almost shapeless and quite primitive lump of organic matter had become sufficiently mature to be called Mr. Mannering at all. These days, which passed quickly enough, in a certain mild, not unpleasant excitement, in the outer world, seemed to the dimly working mind within the bud to resume the whole history of the development of our species, in a great many epochal parts.

A process analogous to the mutations of the embryo was being enacted here. At last the entity which was thus being rushed down an absurdly foreshortened vista of the ages arrived, slowing up, into the foreground. It became recognizable. The Seven Ages of Mr. Mannering were presented, as it were, in a series of close-ups, as in an educational film; his consciousness settled and cleared; the bud was mature, ready to open. At this point, I believe, Mr. Mannering's state of mind was exactly that of a patient, who, struggling up from vague dreams, wakening from under an anæsthetic, asks plaintively, "Where am I?" Then the bud opened, and he knew.

There was the hothouse, but seen from an unfamiliar angle; there, through the glass door, was his study, and there below him was the cat's head (Oh! *Now* he knew.) and there, and there beside him was Cousin Jane. He could not say a word, but then, neither could she. Perhaps it was as well. At the very least, he would have been forced to own that she had been in the right in an argument of long standing; she had always maintained that in the end no good would come of his preoccupation with "those unnatural flowers."

Yet it must be admitted that Mr. Mannering was not at first greatly put out by this extraordinary upheaval in his daily life. This, I think, was partly because he was interested not only in private and personal matters, but in the wider and more general, one might say the biological, aspects of his metamorphosis; as to the rest, simply because he was now a vegetable, he responded with a vegetable reaction. The impossibility of locomotion, for example, did not trouble him in the least, nor even the absence of body and limbs, any more than the cessation of that stream of rashers and tea, biscuits and glasses of milk, luncheon cutlets and so forth that had flowed in at his mouth for over fifty years, but which had now been reversed to a gentle, continuous, scarcely noticeable feeding from below. All the powerful influence of the physical upon the mental, therefore, inclined him towards tranquillity. But the physical is not all. Although no longer a man, he was still Mr. Mannering. Dear me! And from this anomaly, as soon as his scientific interest had subsided, issued a host of woes, mainly subjective in origin.

He was fretted, for instance, by the thought that he would now have no opportunity to name his orchid or to write a paper upon it; and, still worse, there grew up in his mind the abominable conviction that as soon as his plight was discovered, it was he who would be named and classified, and he himself would be the subject of a paper, possibly, even, of comment and criticism in the lay press. Like all orchid collectors, he was excessively shy and sensitive, and in his present situation these qualities brought him to the verge of wilting. Worse yet was the fear of being transplanted, thrust into some unfamiliar, draughty, probably public place. Being dug up! Ugh! A violent shudder pulsated through all the heavy foliage that sprang from Mr. Mannering's division of the plant. He awoke to consciousness of ghostly and remote sensations in the stem below, and in certain tufts of leaves that sprouted from it; they were somehow reminiscent of spine and heart and limbs. He felt quite a dryad.

In spite of all, however, the sunshine was very pleasant. The rich odor of hot spicy earth filled the hothouse. From a special fixture on the hot-water pipes, a little warm steam oozed into the air. Mr. Mannering began to abandon himself to a feeling of *laissez-aller.* Just then, up in the corner of the glass roof, at the ventilator, he heard a persistent buzzing. Soon the note changed from one of irritation to a more complacent sound; a bee had managed to find his way, after some difficulty, through one of the tiny chinks in the metal work. The visitor came drifting down and down through the still, green air, as if into some subaqueous world, and he came to rest on one of those petals which were Mr. Mannering's eyebrows. Thence he commenced to explore one feature after another, and at last he settled heavily on the lower lip, which drooped under his weight and allowed him to crawl right into Mr. Mannering's mouth. This was quite a considerable shock, of course, but on the whole the sensation was neither as alarming nor as unpleasant as might have been expected; indeed, strange as it may sound, the appropriate word seemed to be something like . . . *refreshing.* Perhaps the little tongue had been coated.

But Mr. Mannering soon ceased his drowsy toying with the *mot juste,* when he saw the departed bee, after one or two lazy circlings, settle directly upon the maiden lip of Cousin Jane. Ominous as lightning, a simple botanical principle flashed across the mind of her wretched relative. Which principle? It is only too well known. Even the very babes and sucklings are familiar with it. Is it not drummed into their jaded ears by parents and governesses, curates and the family doctor; is it not Exercise One in the principal subject on the kindergarten curriculum? Cousin Jane was aware of it also, although, being the product of an earlier age, she might have remained still blessedly ignorant had not her cousin, vain, garrulous, proselytizing fool, attempted for years past to interest her in the rudiments of botany. How the miserable man upbraided himself now!

He saw two bunches of leaves just below the flower tremble and flutter and rear themselves painfully upward into the very likeness of two shocked and protesting hands. He saw the soft and orderly petals of his cousin's face ruffle and incarnadine with rage and embarrassment, then turn sickly as a gardenia with horror and dismay. He thought, absurdly enough, of York and Lancaster. But what was he to do? All the rectitude implanted by his careful training, all the chivalry proper to an orchid collector, boiled and surged beneath a paralytically calm exterior. He positively travailed in the effort to activate the muscles of his face, to assume an expression of grief, manly contrition, helplessness in the face of fate, willingness to make all honorable amends, all suffused with the light of a vague but solacing optimism; but it was all in vain. When he had strained till his nerves seemed likely to tear under the tension, the only movement he could achieve was a trivial flutter of the left eyelid—worse than nothing.

This incident completely aroused Mr. Mannering from his vegetable lethargy. He rebelled against the limitations of the form into which he had thus been cast while subjectively he remained all too human. Was he not still at heart a man, with a man's hopes, ideals, aspirations? And capacity for suffering?

When dusk came, and the opulent and sinister shapes of the great plant dimmed to a suggestiveness more powerfully impressive than had been its bright noonday luxuriance, and the atmosphere of a tropical forest filled the orchid house like an exile's dream or the nostalgia of the saxophone, when the cat's whiskers drooped and even Cousin Jane's eyes slowly closed, the unhappy man remained awake, staring into the gathering darkness. Suddenly the light in the study was switched on. Two men entered the room. One of them was his lawyer; the other was his nephew.

"This is his study, as you know, of course," said the wicked nephew. "There's nothing here. I looked round when I came over on Wednesday."

"Ah, well!" said the lawyer. "It's a very queer business, an absolute mystery." He had evidently said so more than once before; they must have been discussing matters in another room. "Well, we must hope for the best. In the meantime, in all the circumstances, it's perhaps as well that you, as next of kin, should take charge of things here. We must hope for the best."

Saying this, the lawyer turned, about to go, and Mr. Mannering saw a malicious smile overspread the young man's face. The uneasiness which had overcome him at first sight of his nephew was intensified to fear and trembling at the sight of this smile.

When he had shown the lawyer out, the nephew returned to the study and looked around with a lively and sinister satisfaction. Then he cut a caper on the hearth-rug. Mr. Mannering thought he had never seen anything so diabolical as this solitary expression of the glee of a venomous nature at the prospect of unchecked sway here whence he had been outcast, license where he had been condemned. How vulgar petty triumph appeared, beheld thus; how disgusting petty spite, how appalling revengefulness and hardness of heart! He remembered suddenly that his nephew had been notable, in his repulsive childhood, for his cruelty to flies, tearing their wings off, and for his barbarity towards cats. A sort of dew might have been noticed upon the good man's forehead. It seemed to him that his nephew had only to glance that way and all would be discovered, although he might have remembered that it was impossible to see from the lighted room into the darkness in the hothouse. His own vision of events inside the room was, of course, only too clear.

On the mantelpiece stood a large unframed photograph of Mr. Mannering. His nephew soon caught sight of this and strode across to confront it with a triumphant and insolent sneer. "What? You old Pharisee," said he, "taken her off for a trip to Brighton, have you? My God! How I hope you'll never come back! How I hope you've fallen over the cliffs, or got swept off by the tide or some-thing! Anyway . . . I'll make hay while the sun shines. Ugh, you old skinflint, you!" And he reached forward his hand, on which the thumb held the middle finger bent and in check, and that finger, when released, rapped viciously upon the nose in the photograph. Then the usurping rascal left the room, and left all the lights on, presumably preferring the dining room with its tantalus and cel-larette to the scholarly austerities of the study.

All night long the glare of electric light from the study fell full upon Mr. Mannering and his Cousin Jane, like the glare of a cheap and artificial sun. You, who have seen at midnight, in the park, a few insomniac asters standing stiff and startled under an arc light, all their weak color bleached out of them by the drenching chemical radiance, neither asleep nor awake, but held fast in a tense, a neurasthenic trance, you can form an idea of how the night passed with this unhappy pair.

And towards morning an incident occurred, trivial in itself, no doubt, but sufficient then and there to add the last drop to poor Cousin Jane's discomfiture, and to her relative's embarrassment and remorse. Along the edge of the great earth-box in which the orchid was planted ran a small black mouse. It had wicked red eyes, a naked, evil snout and huge repellent ears, queer as a bat's. This creature ran straight over the lower leaves of Cousin Jane's part of the plant. It was simply appalling: The stringy main stem writhed like a hair on a coal fire; the leaves contracted in an ag-onized spasm, like seared mimosa; the terrified lady nearly up-rooted herself in her convulsive horror. I think she would actually have done so had not the mouse hurried on past her.

But it had not gone more than a foot or so when it looked up and saw, bending over it, and seeming positively to bristle with life, that flower which had once been called Tib. There was a breathless pause. The mouse was obviously paralyzed with terror; the cat could only look and long. Suddenly the more human watch-ers saw a sly frond of foliage curve softly outward and close in behind the hypnotized creature. Cousin Jane, who had been thinking exultantly, "Well now it'll go away and never, never, never come back," suddenly became aware of hideous possibilities. Summoning all her energy, and you must remember that she had been "out" some days longer than her cousin, and so had much more control of her leaves, she achieved a spasmodic flutter, enough to break the trance that held the mouse, so that, like a clockwork toy, it swung round and fled. But already the fell arm of the orchid had cut off its retreat, the mouse leapt straight at it, like a flash five tendrils at the end caught the fugitive and held it fast, and soon its body dwindled and was gone. Now the heart of Cousin Jane was troubled with horrid fears, and slowly and painfully she turned her weary face first to one side, then to the other, in a fever of anxiety as to where the new bud would appear. A sort of sucker, green and sappy, which twisted lightly about her main stem, and reared a blunt head, much like a tip of asparagus, close to her own, suddenly began to swell in the most suspicious manner. She squinted at it, fascinated and appalled. Could it be her imagination? It was not. . . . But, after all, what are these trifles?

Next evening the door opened again, and again the nephew entered the study. This time he was alone, and it was evident that he had come straight from table. He carried in his hand a decanter of whiskey capped by an inverted glass. Under his arm was a syphon. His face was distinctly flushed, and such a smile as is often seen in saloon bars played about his lips. These lips he occasionally pursed, while simultaneously his cheeks became a little distended; then they would suddenly collapse. He put down his burdens, and, turning to Mr. Mannering's cigar cabinet, produced a bunch of keys which he proceeded to try upon the lock, muttering vindictively at each abortive attempt, until it opened, when he helped himself from the best of its contents. Annoying as it was to witness this insolent appropriation of his property, and mortifying to see the contempt with which the cigar was smoked, the good gentleman found deeper cause for uneasiness in the thought that, with the possession of the keys, his abominable nephew had access to every private corner that was his.

At present, however, the usurper seemed indisposed to carry on investigations; he splashed a great deal of whiskey into the tumbler, and, relaxing into an attitude of extravagant comfort, proceeded to revolt his unseen audience by an exhibition of those animal grossnesses in which a certain type of man is wont to indulge when he fancies himself alone with his Maker. I mean wide, shameless yawning, sucking the teeth, or picking them with a fingernail, eructations, hawking, spitting even. But after a while, the young man began to tire of his own company; he had not yet had time to gather any of his pothouse companions into his uncle's home, and repeated recourse to the whiskey bottle only increased his longing for something to relieve the monotony. His eye fell upon the door of the orchid house. Sooner or later it was bound to have come to pass. Does this thought greatly console the condemned man when the fatal knock sounds upon the door of his cell? No. Nor were the hearts of the trembling pair in the hothouse at all succoured by the reflection.

As the nephew fumbled with the handle of the glass door, Cousin Jane slowly raised two fronds of leaves that grew on each side, high up on her stem, and sank her troubled head behind them. Mr. Mannering observed, in a sudden rapture of hope, that by this device she was fairly well concealed from any casual glance. Hastily he strove to follow her example. Unfortunately, he had not yet gained sufficient control of his—his limbs?—and all his tortured efforts could not raise them beyond an agonized horizontal. The door had opened; the nephew was feeling for the electric light switch just inside. It was a moment for one of the superlative achievements of panic. Mr. Mannering was well equipped for the occasion. Suddenly, at the cost of indescribable effort, he succeeded in raising the right frond, not straight upwards, it is true, but in a series of painful jerks along a curve outward and backward, and ascending by slow degrees till it attained the position of an arm held over the possessor's head from behind. Then, as the light flashed on, a spray of leaves at the very end of this frond spread out into a fan, rather like a very fleshy horse-chestnut leaf in structure, and covered the anxious face below. What a relief! And now the nephew advanced into the orchid house, and now the hidden pair simultaneously remembered the fatal presence of the cat. Simultaneously also, their very sap stood still in their veins. The nephew was walking along by the plant. The cat, a sagacious beast, "knew" with the infallible intuition of its kind that this was an idler, a parasite, a sensualist, gross and brutal, disrespectful to age, insolent to weakness, barbarous to cats. Therefore it remained very still, trusting to its low and somewhat retired position on the plant, and to protective mimicry and such things, and to the half-drunken condition of the nephew, to avoid his notice. But all in vain.

"What?" said the nephew. "What, a cat?" And he raised his hand to offer a blow at the harmless creature. Something in the dignified and unflinching demeanor of this victim must have penetrated into even his besotted mind, for the blow never fell, and the bully, a coward at heart as bullies invariably are, shifted his gaze from side to side to escape the steady, contemptuous stare of the courageous cat. Alas, his eye fell on something glimmering whitely behind the dark foliage. He brushed aside the intervening leaves that he might see what it was. It was Cousin Jane.

"Oh! Ah!" said the young man, in great confusion. "*You're* back. But what are you hiding there for?"

His sheepish stare became fixed, his mouth opened in bewilderment; then the true condition of things dawned upon his mind. Most of us would have at once instituted some attempts at communication, or at assistance of some kind, or at least have knelt down to thank our Creator that we had, by His grace, been spared such a fate, or perhaps have made haste from the orchid house to ensure against accidents. But alcohol had so inflamed the young man's hardened nature that he felt neither fear nor awe nor gratitude, and as for any spirit of helpfulness, that was as far as ever from his hard revengeful heart. As he grasped the situation, a devilish smile overspread his face.

"Ha! Ha! Ha!" said he. "But where's the old man?"

He peered about the plant, looking eagerly for his uncle. In a moment he had located him, and raising the inadequate vizor of leaves, discovered beneath it the face of our hero, troubled with a hundred bitter emotions.

"Hullo, Narcissus!" said the nephew.

A long silence ensued. The nephew was so pleased that he could not say a word. He rubbed his hands together, and licked his lips, and stared and stared as a child might at a new toy.

"You're properly up a tree now," he said. "Yes, the tables are turned now all right, aren't they? Ha! Ha! Do you remember last time we met?"

A flicker of emotion passed over the face of the suffering blossom, betraying consciousness.

"Yes, you can hear what I say," added the tormentor. "Feel too, I expect. What about that?"

As he spoke, he stretched out his hand, and, seizing a delicate frill of fine, silvery filaments that grew as whiskers grow round the lower half of the flower, he administered a sharp tug. The result would have interested that ingenious experimenter Sir J. C. Bose. Without pausing to note, however, even in the interests of science, the subtler shades of his uncle's reaction, content with the general effect of that devastating wince, the wretch chuckled with satisfaction, and, taking a long pull from the reeking butt of the stolen cigar, puffed the vile fumes straight into his victim's centre. The brute!

"How do you like that, John the Baptist?" he asked with a leer. "Good for the blight, you know. Just what you want!"

Something rustled upon his coat sleeve. Looking down, he saw a long stalk, well adorned with the fatal tendrils, groping its way over the arid and unsatisfactory surface. In a moment it had reached his wrist; he felt it fasten, but knocked it off as one would a leech, before it had time to establish its hold.

"Ugh!" said he. "So that's how it happens, is it? I think I'll keep outside till I get the hang of things a bit. I don't want to be made an Aunt Sally of. Though I shouldn't think they could get you with your clothes on." Struck by a sudden thought, he looked from his uncle to Cousin Jane, and from Cousin Jane back to his uncle again. He scanned the floor, and saw a single crumpled bath-towel robe lying in the shadow.

"Why," he said, "*well!* . . . Haw! Haw! Haw!" And with an odious backward leer, he made his way out of the orchid house.

Mr. Mannering felt that his suffering was capable of no increase. Yet he dreaded the morrow. His fevered imagination patterned the long night with waking nightmares, utterly fantastic visions of humiliation and torture. Torture! It was absurd, of course, for him to fear cold-blooded atrocities on the part of his nephew, but how he dreaded some outrageous whim that might tickle the youth's sense of humor and lead him to *any* wanton freak, especially if he were drunk at the time. He thought of slugs and snails, espaliers and topiary. Oh! Oh! Oh! If only the monster would rest content with insults and mockery, with wasting his substance, ravaging his cherished possessions before his eyes, with occasional pulling at the whiskers, even! Then it might be possible to turn gradually from all that still remained in him of man, to subdue the passions, no longer to admire or desire, to go native, as it were, relapsing into the Nirvana of a vegetable dream. But in the morning he found this was not so easy.

In came the nephew, and, pausing only to utter the most perfunctory of jeers at his relatives in the glass house, he sat at the desk and unlocked the top drawer. He was evidently in search of money, his eagerness betrayed that; no doubt he had run through all he had filched from his uncle's pockets and had not yet worked out a scheme for getting direct control of his bank account. However, the drawer held enough to cause the scoundrel to rub his hands with satisfaction, and, summoning the housekeeper, to bellow into her ear a reckless order upon the wine and spirits merchant.

"Get along with you," he shouted, when he had at last made her understand. "I shall have to get someone a bit more on the spot to wait on me! I can tell you that. Yes," he added to himself as the poor old woman hobbled away, deeply hurt by his bullying manner, "yes, a nice little parlor maid . . . a nice little parlor maid."

He hunted in the Buff Book for the number of the local registry office. That afternoon he interviewed a succession of maidservants in his uncle's study. Those that happened to be plain, or too obviously respectable, he treated curtly and coldly; they soon made way for others. It was only when a girl was attractive (according to the young man's depraved tastes, that is) and also bore herself in a fast or brazen manner that the interviews were at all prolonged. In these cases the nephew would conclude in a fashion that left no doubt at all in the minds of any of his auditors as to his real intentions. Once, for example, leaning forward, he took the girl by the chin, saying with an odious smirk, "There's no one else but me, and so you'd be treated just like one of the family; d'you see, my dear?" To another he would say, slipping his arm round her waist, "Do you think we shall get on well together? Will you make me nice and cozy and comfortable, eh?" He addressed one as "Baby," another as "Chicken." I can't imagine what poor Cousin Jane must have thought.

After this conduct had sent two or three in confusion from the room, there entered a young person of the most regrettable description, one whose character, betrayed as it was in her meretricious finery, her crude cosmetics and her tinted hair, showed yet more clearly in florid gesture and too facile smile. The nephew lost no time in coming to an arrangement with this creature. Indeed, her true nature was so obvious that the depraved young man only went through the farce of an ordinary interview as a sauce to his anticipations, enjoying the contrast between conventional dialogue and unbridled glances. She was to come next day. Mr. Mannering feared more for his unhappy cousin than for himself. "What scenes may she not have to witness," he thought, "that yellow cheek of hers to incarnadine?" If only he could have said a few words!

But that evening, when the nephew came to take his ease in the study, it was obvious that he was far more under the influence of liquor than had been the case before. His face, flushed patchily by the action of the spirits, wore a sullen sneer, an ominous light burned in that bleared eye, he muttered savagely under his breath. Clearly this fiend in human shape was what is known as "fighting drunk"; clearly some trifle had set his vile temper in a blaze.

It is interesting to note, even at this stage, a sudden change in Mr. Mannering's reactions. They now seemed entirely egotistical and were to be elicited only by stimuli directly associated with physical matters. The nephew kicked a hole in a screen in his drunken fury, he flung a burning cigar end down on the carpet, he scratched matches on the polished table. His uncle witnessed this with the calm of one whose sense of property and of dignity has become numbed and paralyzed; he felt neither fury nor mortification. Had he, by one of those sudden strides by which all such development takes place, approached much nearer to his goal, complete vegetation? His concern for the threatened modesty of Cousin Jane, which had moved him so strongly only a few hours earlier, must have been the last dying flicker of exhausted altruism; that most human characteristic had faded from him. He felt that relief which certain sick people feel when they first notice the influence of a drug as an irregular blur on their consciousness of pain, or which unhappy lovers enjoy when they first rub their hands and skip about the room in a morning ecstasy of (probably illusory) indifference. But instead of running to the glass and rapturously greeting himself as a long-lost friend, as this latter class generally does, Mr. Mannering soberly prepared to bid his personality farewell. The change, however, in its present stage, was not an unmixed blessing. Narrowing in from the wider and more expressly human regions of his being, his consciousness now felt outside its focus not only pride and altruism, which had been responsible for much of his woe, but fortitude and detachment also, which, with quotation from the Greeks, had been his support before the whole battery of his distresses. Moreover, within its constricted circle, his ego was not reduced, but concentrated; his serene, flowerlike indifference towards the ill-usage of his furniture was balanced by the absorbed, flowerlike single-mindedness of his terror at the thought of similar ill-usage directed towards himself. It is important now to appreciate this white, intense light of Mr. Mannering's apprehensions.

What a strange shock it would be, if, shall we say, in the third act of *Hamlet,* the mind, dispread in contemplation of diverse forces converging harmoniously on some still-distant consummation, were suddenly *jabbed* (as a sea anemone by a stick) by the spectacle of the King treading by chance upon Hamlet's toe and causing him such annoyance that in a flash . . .

Inside the study the nephew still fumed and swore. On the mantelpiece stood an envelope, addressed in Mr. Mannering's handwriting to Cousin Jane. In it was the letter he had written from town, describing his nephew's disgraceful conduct. The young man's eye fell upon this, and, unscrupulous, impelled by idle curiosity, he took it up and drew out the letter. As he read, his face grew a hundred times blacker than before.

"What?" he muttered. " '. . . a mere race-course cad . . . a worthless vulgarian . . . a scoundrel of the sneaking sort' . . . And what's this? . . . 'cut him off absolutely' . . . What?" said he, with a horrifying oath. "*Would* you cut me off absolutely? Two can play at that game, you old devil!"

And he snatched up a large pair of scissors that lay on the desk and burst into the hothouse.

Among fish, the dory, they say, screams when it is seized upon by man; among insects, the caterpillar of the death's-head moth is capable of a still, small shriek of terror. In the vegetable world, only the mandrake could voice its agony—till now.